THE CONFESSIONS

OF

PRESTON AND TAYLOR

A Ghetto Love Story with a Twist

by MARQUIS "POOH" DUNN

The Confessions of Preston and Taylor

Pres.tig.ious Publications

Copyright 2025 by Marquis "Pooh" Dunn

Dedications

Glory be to my Lord and Savior, Jesus Christ, for blessing me with another opportunity to reach the masses with my words. I would like to dedicate this book to my loving auntie Patricia "Aunt Pat" Wiseman, my brother/partner in many crimes Marshall "Bay Bay" Adkins, and a very special and uniquely beautiful pair of sisters who always placed a huge smile on my face every single time I saw or heard their voices, "Ms. Maxine," "Ms. Ruby Dee," "Coffee and Desiree "Desi" Johnson." May you all rest peacefully in Heaven. Much Love, Marquis "Pooh Sheisty" Dunn, as Ms. Ruby Dee would say... lol.

Acknowledgements

First and foremost, allow me to give all glory and praise to the one who consistently keeps making all of this doable and possible – which is my Lord and Savior, Jesus Christ. Without Him, there is honestly no telling what else I'd probably be attempting right now. So, thank you, Lord, for not only keeping me focused but also for giving me the sound judgment and additional strength of staying on the right path. Only you know how difficult that is for me to do at times, especially with temptation constantly lurking and looming on every corner.

Secondly, I would like to thank God for perseverance, endurance, and faith.

And most importantly, I would like to thank all of my true supporters who not only loved, appreciated, and physically read my first two books, but also took the time out of their busy days to share their thoughts, elations, and opinions with me in the most honest of ways. So, thank you all, because you're the reason that I constantly stay inspired to share my views with the world on such a regular basis.

And last but not least, I would like to give a major, major shoutout to me!! For never giving up… never accepting defeat… and for never allowing anything or anybody to discourage the dreams in which God has planted deeply within my spirit!! No matter how hard some tend to try!

P.S. Tee, we've done it again, homie!!

Shout out to all of my other brothers & sisters that are locked behind those walls as well... stay focused, stay hopeful, stay prayed up, and keep fighting!! No matter how dim certain days may appear to be.

Much Love,

Marquis "Pooh" Dunn

THE CONFESSIONS

OF

PRESTON AND TAYLOR

A Ghetto Love Story with a Twist

Introduction

With jealousy, envy, deception, and several blatant acts of betrayal unfolding on the behalf of so many different individuals, Preston and Taylor both do their darndest to navigate all of the many pitfalls that encompass them from every angle, corner, or side. The journey forces the two strangers closer together somehow in this excitingly twisted and highly dysfunctional series of events, where nobody is really who they say they are, and love or loyalty only appears to be a façade! Especially from those closest to you.

Welcome to the Confessions of Preston and Taylor, "A Ghetto Love Story with a Twist!"

Chapter 1

Taylor was a wholesome young lady blessed with a very good upbringing. She and her sisters were raised under the same roof with both of her parents, Mark and Jezebel, which was highly unlikely for most African American children. Because of this, Taylor believed that she had firsthand knowledge of what black love actually looked like.

Or so she thought. But she would soon learn just how wrong she was.

Taylor was far too young and naive to recognize all of the smokescreens and pretentious facades her parents had customarily created amongst themselves, solely for the sake of their children's happiness. Taylor didn't see the truth hidden behind their smiles. And this time, the man wasn't the one to blame.

Taylor's mother was a very beautiful woman, just like her daughters. They were blessed to inherit their mother's striking beauty, quick-witted intellect, and alluring physique. Jezebel had long, silky hair with long, sexy legs, like those of a runway model, but with the muscular build of a track star, along with nearly every attention-grabbing attribute known to man. And she flaunted it with arrogance.

Jezebel was every man's ideal fantasy and every jealous woman's nightmare, and she knew it. She capitalized on it, just as many other beautiful women had done throughout history. But that, of course, is another story.

Taylor was the middle child of her siblings. This caused her to have many different emotions, from good to great. Good that she was somebody's big sister, or so-called overseer, and great that she was her father's favorite. As far as their appearance was concerned, Taylor and Mark looked to be identical.

Mark, Taylor's father, was an extremely astute man. Dead serious while amongst men other than his family or closest friends, but a complete teddy bear when it came to dealing with his daughters. And Taylor was his heart, just as he was hers.

They could do no wrong in each other's eyes, and everyone in the family knew it. This unspoken bond caused a small twinge of jealousy between her and her sisters, but also within the heart of her mother. And that jealousy eventually led to her mother's infidelity with other men.

Her infidelity with other men unraveled the final seams of their so-called happy marriage. That was something Taylor, nor the rest of her family, could ever seem to forgive. Jezebel's infidelity with other men broke her father, eventually deteriorating his once perfectly clean bill of health, until he finally passed away from an unrecognizable heartache, better known as *Broken Heart syndrome.*

That is also the one thing that Taylor has constantly struggled with every single day since the funeral director slowly lowered her father's body into the ground.

Chapter 2

"What up homie, what it do?" Preston asked his most loyal comrade and best friend, Mystique, as he stepped foot onto the block for the first time that day. He carefully scanned the faces of every passing car within a hundred-foot radius, looking for any and everything out of the ordinary as he mentally prepared himself for what he expected to be another extensively profitable day in the streets.

"Nothing much, bruh. Same ole' same with me, dawg, ya feel me. What's up with you, though?" Mystique replied, thumbing through a large sum of cash without missing a beat. He gave Preston dap, then handed him the money.

Preston quickly slipped it into the back pocket of his jeans, making sure to keep it separate from all of the other bankrolls he'd previously collected that day. He had a process to keep up with all of the money he collected. When it came down to Preston's dividends, he didn't play, and the streets knew this firsthand!

Preston was smooth. Cooler than the other side of the pillow, as the old heads used to say. Above all else, he

4

was real! He was really mature, really respectful, and extremely intelligent. Preston was a Hustler. A bona fide Hustler, to be exact. He loved crunching numbers, fixing problems, and solving equations, not just for himself, but for those he loved and cared for the most. Which appeared to be almost everybody, especially his people of African descent.

Preston was a thinker. A deep thinker. A true connoisseur of strategy, as he sometimes liked to call himself. And he loved it! Almost as much as he loved creating countless arduous situations for himself just to dissect, study, and overanalyze every inch of the problem from beginning to end. He forced his mind to evaluate each situation from every possible angle with much precision, exploring every angle until he finally reached a solution.

Recognizing these gifts within Preston, the neighborhood's movers and shakers started calling him "Sol," short for Solution. No matter how difficult the task, Preston almost always appeared to come up with an answer.

Analyzing Preston from afar, you might assume, like most police enforcement did, that he was some sort of dealer. Heroin dealer, cocaine dealer, weapons dealer, etc. But neither of these extracurricular activities was his thing.

To be honest, Preston was a pimp. Not in the sense of actually manipulating or abusing females for capital, but definitely in the sense of acquiring knowledge, wisdom, and all sorts of other very pertinent types of life-altering information on the so-called upper echelons of the city.

He collected secrets that were not only capable of destroying the lives of certain individuals, but also those of their closest loved ones, colleagues, and family members as well. And those very secrets were now paying Preston a king's ransom, far more than any uncut drug, any weapon, or any exotic fleet of high-end call girls ever could. And the massive amount of currency that Mystique forked over to Preston, his partner in crime, was a prime example of this very fact.

Preston and Mystique had been partners from the womb. Their bond was unshakable, and it wasn't a bond on God's green earth more solid than theirs.

Their brotherhood had been battle-tested on multiple fronts, and nothing or no one had ever been able to penetrate its validity. Not even trumped-up murder and conspiracy to commit murder charges. Which were the very charges that landed them in the "clink," as some would call it, for several long years of their young lives before they finally beat the cases and were released.

And it was all accomplished by them both remaining solid, never talking to detectives, and forever staying loyal to each other. Something that both men religiously practiced and sacredly believed in since they were kids because they were definitely each other's keeper, and that was a fact, regardless of how the chips may have attempted to fall.

Chapter 3

With her father gone, the light in Taylor's once bubbly spirit had quickly begun to dim. Her mother's callous demeanor and blatantly distasteful behavior towards her child only magnified Taylor's sadness even more.

Depression couldn't even begin to describe Taylor's current state of mind. Nor did the word suicidal. She had mentally surpassed both of those extremely fragile phases within her mind. The gloomy expression that adorned her once extremely attractive appearance was all the evidence needed to determine this fact. The pain was etched in her face for all to see.

There was no way on earth that Taylor could ever begin to conceal her natural beauty. But the confidence that it took to embrace such powerful traits had now vanished. The only thing that kept any remaining embers of light burning deeply within her soul was remembering the mesmerizing gaze of her father's eyes. But even those memories were becoming vague and short-lived.

Unable to muster up enough inner strength to stop the constant flow of tears cascading down her cheeks,

Taylor stared at herself in the mirror, vividly visualizing her father's handsome face, as she studied her own appearance. She abruptly turned away from the mirror in hopes of ridding her mind of all the painful images entirely. She fell to her knees, steadily conversing with her father as if he were still there, sobbing harder with every word.

"Daddy, why? Why, Daddy? Why! Why would you leave me down here all by myself with this crazy woman? Daddy, how could you do this to me!"

Taylor profusely sobbed like the brokenhearted little girl that she was.

She prayed to God as she conversed with her deceased father, all in the same breath. She asked them both to supply her with the strength it would take for her to make it through this extremely tumultuous situation.

And for the will to live without her father.

She never expected her prayer would be answered by God so soon, in the form of a peculiar young man known as Preston, a.k.a. "Young Sol."

Chapter 4

Witnessing a small crowd of people slowly congregating in the grocery store parking lot of 922 Place, Taylor skeptically strolled by, with much apprehension, casting her head downward to avoid any possible eye contact. Not out of fear, but from the weight of lost confidence that had overtaken her once extremely overconfident demeanor. She did everything within her power to remain inconspicuous as she hurriedly increased her pace.

Mrs. Maxine stood on the front porch of her apartment building, keeping a close eye on the young men she had raised as if they were her own, making sure they were perfectly fine. She fully understood just how quickly her community could go from being peaceful to complete mayhem in the blink of an eye, especially when crooked cops or any other outside entities presented themselves as a threat to them in any type of way.

Upon closer observation, Mrs. Maxine noticed the young lady who was subtly trying to make her way past the rowdy group of young teenage men and emphatically barked at the crowd for blocking the walkway. Hearing her demands was all it took for them to clear the path for Taylor to pass.

Taylor slightly raised her head, enough to vaguely make eye contact, and kindly mouthed a silent "thank you" to the older, attractive woman with the meticulously cropped and professionally styled hairdo. In her mind, Mrs. Maxine didn't look a day over forty, though Taylor knew she was older.

Mrs. Maxine respectively reciprocated the young lady's pleasantries with a kind smile and a slight head nod as if to say, "Don't mention it." After realizing that everything was copacetic, she pivoted and dashed back inside her home to catch the last remaining parts of "Days of Our Lives." Her favorite television soap opera. Because *there was no telling what Victor Kiriakis, Sami Brady, or Stefano DiMera had up their sleeves,* Mrs. Maxine thought to herself. She was almost more than positive that they were definitely up to no good, and she wasn't about to miss another second of their treachery if she could help it.

Mrs. Maxine reclaimed her favorite spot on the living room sofa while comfortably propping her feet upon the coffee table, just as Bo Brady was once again attempting to rescue Hope after being kidnapped by the dastardly and very conniving Ernesto Toscano.

"That's right, Bo. Go get your woman back, boy! Go get her back from that low-down dog!" Mrs. Maxine passionately yelled at the television screen with much enthusiasm.

Unbeknownst to her, she would soon be witnessing some of these very same events play out right before her very own eyes between Preston and Taylor. A series full of episodes that even Bo and Hope Brady would envy if their love affair really existed.

Chapter 5

Preston was the first to take heed to Mrs. Maxine's demands. He slowly eased himself and a few of his comrades away from the sidewalk, giving Taylor all of the access she needed in order to safely pass by the rambunctious bunch of young teens. And he was glad he did because it gave him a much better view of Taylor's beauty up close, which momentarily took his breath away.

Her beauty caused something mysteriously bizarre to occur within the depths of Preston's innermost deepest intercostal muscles that had never happened before, especially not due to the presence of a woman. His rapidly palpitating heartbeat somehow consistently aligned with that of his now highly irregular pulse. All sorts of unsolicited sensations suddenly traveled to Preston's brain from every possible direction, even long after Taylor had made it completely around the corner.

He unconsciously nodded his head up and down as if he was answering his very own questions racing through his mind. Preston tried to convince himself that whatever he was thinking about in that moment was true. Oblivious to the jokes that were being hurled his way by Mystique and the rest of the fellows, Preston absentmindedly continued to stare up the street for a second or two longer before finally snapping back to reality.

But only partially. For the life of him, Preston just couldn't rid his psyche of the intoxicating glare or the shape of the beautiful young stranger's eyes. No matter how hard he tried.

Trying to play it cool, Preston playfully threw several different combinations of punches towards every laughing and snickering face that surrounded him in an attempt to divert the onslaught of jokes that were continuously coming his way. Preston started to laugh and finally tossed his hands up in defeat.

"Y'all got me, man... y'all got me," Preston admitted, suddenly cracking a few funny jokes of his own.

He began roasting the two main individuals, Mystique and Jermaine, who were mostly responsible for all of the laughs and jokes in the first place. They were two of the funniest dudes that ever existed on planet earth from Preston's perspective. Although neither one of them ever really talked much.

The trio went back and forth with one another for what appeared to be an eternity, and they loved each and every single moment of the show. The crowd managed to grow larger and larger in size with every joke.

Preston and Mystique held their own in the beginning, but were no match for the quick-witted, slick-tongued comedic skills of Jermaine. He verbally battled both men, joke for joke, until a few of the onlookers fell to the ground clutching their stomachs, releasing several droplets of urine. Which, at this point, was more than physically obvious due to the visible pee-pee stains that resided on the crotch area of their garments.

And all of them weren't men either.

Multiple women wet themselves, which made everything that much funnier to everyone present. The little pissers hurriedly scrambled away in search of the closest bathroom, the whole time steadily laughing and pissing themselves even more with little to no type of embarrassment of any kind. They scrambled away, thanking each individual by name, which only made everyone laugh that much harder.

As the crowd slowly began to disperse, they continued with their normal scheduled lives as if nothing had ever happened, right along with Preston and the rest of the fellows.

The crew got back to business, planning a huge neighborhood barbecue to include a special prize giveaway for the entire community to enjoy. This was their way of giving back to the people whom they loved, protected, and cared for most of all. They bickered with one another about who was gonna pay for what. Not in a bad way, but because each of them wanted to show their love and respect more than the next man by paying for the entire event themselves. When everything was all said and done, they laughed and decided to equally share the cost.

But Preston's mind once again drifted off, thinking about the beautiful, young stranger that he had *not really encountered* earlier that day but had very much seen. He was hoping and praying to himself to see her again really soon.

If she were still around, that is, Preston thought, looking back up the street in the direction that Taylor had previously walked just one last time, in hopes of stealing another glimpse of her beautiful face, as his heart continuously pounded within his chest in quick succession.

Chapter 6

Taylor tossed and turned in her sleep throughout the night, as did Preston. But for two very different reasons.

Taylor's restlessness came from the recurring dreams that she constantly had night after night since the devastating passing of her father. But also from the absence of love that she felt from the woman who was supposedly her mother, who, in turn, had never truthfully acted like a mother at all, from Taylor's perspective, which often kept her in tears.

Preston's struggles, on the other hand, were nowhere near as severe as Taylor's. But they were still tormenting to his spirit all the same. He couldn't seem to think of anything or anyone else, besides the immensely beautiful stranger with the deeply saddened eyes. That concerned him.

Preston lay in bed on his back, staring at the ceiling with his hands casually clasped behind his cranium in deep thought. He did everything under the sun to keep from enjoying the pleasantries of the tall girl's breathtakingly beautiful appearance, which, at the moment, was deemed almost impossible for him to do as he desperately fought against releasing an extremely huge smile. But to no avail, of course.

Preston grinned, accepting what was blooming inside of him, no longer fighting against the incredible feelings that the stranger had somehow rendered. Which was more than oddly strange and very uncommon for him. Uncommon, just as the tantalizing beauty that the young lady possessed had also been for him as well.

Preston dropped down to the floor to knock out several quick sets of push-ups, perfectly executing the exercises with a full range of motion. He was hoping that this tactic would be more than effective in making him extremely fatigued so that he could fall back asleep.

"One... two... three... four... five... six...," Preston consistently pushed.

He repeatedly pumped out push-up after push-up until his chest and triceps muscles were highly inflamed with a sudden influx of blood, causing them to bulge out and physically show, which Preston loved.

Pausing in between sets and remaining on the floor, Preston began to flex a little. Admiring his physique, he looked around for anything that would show off his reflection. Before he realized it, he had done hundreds of push-ups, and he planned to do hundreds more before it was all said and done. So he thought.

But his body had chosen a different agenda.

Somewhere in between his last sct of push-ups and the thought of him attempting to do some more, he finally drifted back to sleep on the carpeted surface. Mentally and physically exhausted, Preston was abnormally snoring loudly, as he somewhat shook the pavement.

"Huugggh… Huugggh… Huugggh!"

Chapter 7

The next morning started absolutely amazing for Taylor. She felt extremely energized and refreshed, though she wasn't sure why. The smells that were emitting from her grandmother's kitchen added to her elation even more.

She hurriedly climbed out of bed to wash her face and brush her teeth so she could go assist her GiGi in the kitchen with the remainder of the cooking. That was something Taylor loved doing with her grandmother ever since she was a child.

Memories of those moments made Taylor's day even better, bringing an even bigger smile to her face, which resembled the same smile that she had fallen asleep with the night before while visualizing her father's handsome face. A face that was the carbon copy of that of her very own, shape for shape, crease for crease, and linc for line. Now that all the bags and puffiness underneath her eyes had vanished, that resemblance felt even stronger.

She smiled proudly at her reflection in the mirror, revealing perfectly aligned pearly white teeth and high cheekbones passed down from her father's side, a blessing she appreciated. Flirting with herself in the mirror, she winked at her reflection and laughed.

Taylor finished pampering herself while humming along to one of her grandmother's favorite tunes. The soulful sounds of Anita Baker's "Angel" loudly blared from the living room speakers, filling the whole house with a love that could only be resonated with that of her GiGi's home. Taylor smoothly crooned her way into her grandmother's kitchen, planting a soft kiss on her cheek.

Taylor got to work immediately after washing her hands for a second time. She whisked and seasoned the eggs just as GiGi had taught her to do. She scrambled them to perfection until they became light and fluffy, then added the appropriate amount of sharp cheddar cheese.

For her, the cheese was definitely the secret ingredient that allowed the eggs to simply melt in your mouth. She scooped out a small portion from the skillet to give GiGi a tester.

"Well done, baby girl... well done," GiGi replied. "Now go put 'em in that bowl over there on the counter, and set 'em on the table with the rest of the food lil girl, because I'm starving. And tell everyone else that I said to wash their hands and get their behinds down them stairs as well. Because I'm only praying over this food one time!" GiGi stated as she turned back to add the finishing touches to the fried potatoes and onions. She removed them from the cast-iron skillet, then took her seat right next to the head of the table. A place that she had always left vacant since the passing of her son.

GiGi dabbed the corner of her eyes while staring at the picture of Mark, Taylor, Taylor's sisters, and Mark's no-good wife, Jezebel - the only person of her son's so called immediate family who was no longer welcomed to set foot inside of the comforts of GiGi's home ever again.

And she meant that with all of her heart!

Chapter 8

Jezebel, Taylor's mother, appeared to be the least bit fazed by the passing of her late husband, Mark. And even less concerned about the well-being of her children, especially Taylor, whom she hadn't physically laid eyes upon since before her father's funeral procession.

And to be honest about the entire situation, she couldn't care less about any of it at all.

Jezebel collected the substantial lump sum of life insurance money from her ex-husband's policy. Rumors said it was anywhere from several hundred thousand to well over a million dollars. And it was rumored that she was living it up to the fullest.

She had nothing on her mind at the time except for herself, her newly opened bank account, and the fresh new piece of young meat that she'd acquired a week or two before her late husband's death. Her new man was barely older than her oldest daughter. And Jezebel was enjoying each and every inch of him.

She greedily sized him up, vividly imagining what she wanted to do to him in that moment, reflecting on the night before that had been nothing less than amazing for her. She tightly clenched her thighs together in hopes of controlling the juices that were flowing to the center of her panty liner from the thoughts of their last encounter. She tried to shift her thoughts, but the grin upon her attractive face expressed her true satisfaction with no shame.

Jezebel was more than disrespectful in her actions, gleefully parading her young trophy throughout the city without a single solitary care in the world. Constantly flaunting massive wads of cash around town for everyone to see, with her young lover attached to her hip, spending up as much of her late husband's riches as he possibly could.

Spending her money suited him just fine. Especially since all Jezebel wanted from him in return was for him to simply keep her satisfied and feeling young, if you know what I mean.

Or so he naively believed.

He seductively slapped the extremely attractive, much older Jezebel on her perfectly round buttocks while his eyes filled with lust as he watched it jiggle and bounce. He eased in close, invading her personal space, allowing her to feel his full erection. She seductively looked back in his direction and quickly approved of his actions with a wink and a smile.

Subtly disguising this as love in the most broken way possible from each of their perspectives. They both used and manipulated one another, which were the main commonalities that drew these two troubled spirits together in the first place.

Both parties fully understood that love would never exist between them in this extremely toxic example of a lie that they called a relationship. They both appeared to be more than overly satisfied with their acts of deception towards one another and living a lie without any regrets. But most importantly, they were absolutely satisfied with the sex!

Sex was the only thing that always drew them both closer together with every lust-filled thrust during their many wild and very adventurous bouts of fornication.

It was a tool that they each used to manipulate and acquire almost everything they had ever needed, desired, and yearned for during the course of their lives. Which was mainly money, power, and respect. But most importantly, control!

The only problem was that they were both attempting to run those same manipulatively deceptive games on one another now.

So the million-dollar question is: Which of these two disloyal and very conniving varmints will be victorious?

Would it be youth over beauty, or fresh new blood over old cougar?

Which would you choose?

Chapter 9

The sounds of spoons, knives, and forks clinking and scraping against plates and bowls filled GiGi's home. The sounds all skillfully blended together with the synchronized smacking and chewing from several different-size sets of lips, mysteriously creating a rhythm like the opening to an old James Brown classic.

Several deep breaths, loud sighs, and a plethora of grunts from full bellies added to this harmonious occasion. Many elated gestures of satisfaction fondly replaced any existence of words, leaving absolutely no room for conversation of any kind. GiGi pleasantly smiled at each of her relatives surrounding her at the dining room table. Immeasurably filling her heart with joy.

It had been quite a while since this much love and affection filled the walls of her humble abode, GiGi thought, smiling even broader than ever before. When she got up to throw away her scraps, she was stopped in her tracks by one of her grandchildren, then suddenly told to relax.

"Take a seat, GiGi, I got it." Taylor's youngest sibling quickly suggested, who, at the time, also felt enamored and affected by the present euphoria of GiGi's home.

This feeling was something that each of them had been missing and desperately longing for, for quite some time now. Especially since the current passing of their father.

Taylor gently pulled each of her relatives into an affectionate group hug, with GiGi and her sisters being closest to her body. Everyone, men, women, children, shed a few tears for Mark - their father, son, brother, uncle, or cousin. All in the name of love.

"GiGi, I love you!" Taylor genuinely expressed to her grandmother as their family embrace finally came to an end, laughing and joking the entire time while still smothering their grandmother with kisses from every direction. GiGi loved the affection, and it clearly showed.

Taylor basked in the moment for a second or two longer. She gladly watched and admired the scene unfold before grabbing the trash bag full of garbage and heading for the front door.

Exiting the home, she was greeted by the slight ruggedness of the attractive stranger from the day before, bumping into him. She never expected anyone to be at the entrance of her GiGi's door.

"Excuse me, Ms. Lady, I didn't mean to startle you," Preston pleasantly stated, reaching out towards Taylor to keep her from falling. Taylor dropped the garbage bag, and Preston reached for it and picked it up.

Taking out the trash was something he'd been faithfully doing for GiGi and several more of the elders within the community, just so that they wouldn't have to.

"Move, dude. I got it!" Taylor vehemently exclaimed. She shrewdly brushed past Preston, more so out of embarrassment than out of anger. She sensed he could feel how enamored she had become just from the sight of him.

Or so she thought.

Taylor quickly discarded the trash from her hand and into the garbage bin with much unnecessary force, but she never once looked back in the stranger's direction. Figuring that he was still watching her every move, Taylor's heart rapidly pounded within her chest like the deep vibrations of a high school bass drum.

"Boom Boom! Boom Boom! Boom Boom!"

It was the exact same thing that Preston's heart had been doing as well, ever since the day he first laid eyes on Taylor when she walked past him on the street.

And now he knew exactly why. It was because of the young lady that Ms. GiGi referred to as "Taylor," and to him, she was absolutely gorgeous.

Mean scowl and all.

Chapter 10

Taylor had finally found a secluded spot not far from her GiGi's home to hide out. Still feeling hesitant and slightly embarrassed by her earlier behavior, she was adamant about not running into the attractive stranger again. And she meant it.

"But he was kinda cute though," Taylor admitted to herself, shyly giggling and covering her mouth. A wave of butterflies danced in her stomach as if performing the twine, the world-renowned line dance beloved in the Black community, especially at weddings, barbecues, and nightclubs. No other group could do it better, and that was a fact. Taylor knew that Black people had always been the creators, teachers, trendsetters, and the foundation of culture and civilization as we currently know it today. No matter how hard white America tried to erase or hide that truth, she knew better. They couldn't hide the real truths of her people's prominence in the world.

The thought made her smile widen as she leaned her head against the brick wall she was using as a protective shield, closing her eyes and soaking in the images of her previous thoughts, until someone rudely disrupted it all by disrespectfully kicking her foot.

"What are you doing back here by yourself, girl? Who are you waiting on?" asked Duck, her extremely irritating big cousin. He eyed her suspiciously, assuming she was sneaking off to meet some knuckle-headed neighborhood boy behind GiGi's back. "Not on my watch," he said, quickly ushering her back to the front of the house, the very place she had been avoiding.

"I hope he's gone… I hope he's gone… I hope he's gone," Taylor chanted. She did not want to face the attractive stranger and inaudibly mumbled underneath her breath the whole time, shuffling her feet back towards the front behind her big cousin Duck in an attempt to stall.

Duck was growing more agitated with her, convinced she was being secretive about some knuckle-headed little boy. And honestly, he wasn't wrong, but not in the way he imagined. Taylor bent down for the third time to retie her already-tied shoe, still silently chanting underneath her breath, "I hope he's gone… I hope he's gone... I hope he's gone!"

Chapter 11

Preston had replayed the brief meet and greet with Taylor a hundred times. Or maybe more. And, for the life of him, he still couldn't understand what had just happened between them, and it threw him completely off balance. Scratching his head in confusion, he struggled to make sense of what was going on in his brain.

To be honest, this incident was discombobulating and more than extremely odd to him, which disturbed his normally cool, calm, and collected train of thought in the worst way possible. Leaving him even more confused than he'd been with their very first interaction with one another.

Still, it wasn't enough to dissuade him.

Preston started mentally preparing for what was to come. He knew that capturing Taylor's attention, let alone keeping it, was not going to be an easy thing for him to do. But that was just how he liked it. Preston had been taught by the elders in his community, and he believed that anything worth having or that was worth keeping came with a price. And judging by what he saw in Taylor, she was absolutely worth it.

An even larger smile appeared upon his handsome face. Preston loved a challenge and was truly admiring the fact that God seemed to be presenting him with yet another major obstacle through the likes of Taylor.

Preston thought she may be one of his most difficult feats ever up until that point. He had no idea just how true that would turn out to be.

Preston was not one to be denied, and he meant every word he said, as his confidence began to resonate within his spirit. This caused him to take cooler and smoother strides back towards the bottom of Georgia Court Avenue, where Mystique and the rest of the fellows congregated, laughing, joking, shooting dice, and throwing horseshoes amongst a multitude of many other miscellaneous neighborhood activities.

All in the name of making a dollar.

To them, that hustle was justified. Their circumstances demanded it, due to their impoverished living conditions and environmental circumstances.

Or at least that's what they all believed.

But no one outside that life could ever truly understand. Society either ignored their reality or pretended it didn't exist. Especially when it came to Black folks, Preston thought.

He brushed off thoughts of Taylor and focused on the situation unfolding ahead. Mystique looked tense, brows furrowed. Something was wrong.

"What is it now?" Preston muttered to himself. Preston slightly shook his head in disbelief even before receiving any information from Mystique.

Preston recited a quick prayer, asking God to prepare his steps in that moment and to give him the guidance he needed to properly assess, and hopefully resolve, the entire situation as rapidly as possible. He joined Mystique, Lil Gary, his big cousins, M&M, and Jermaine, Rell, and Bay on the corner by Mrs. Maxine's apartment building, ready to mediate whatever it was that was going on between them. From the looks of things, with all of their blatantly agitated and extremely disturbed compositions, he quickly determined they definitely needed some assistance.

Preston gathered himself as best as he could before releasing a small sigh. He attentively listened to Bay and the rest of his partners as they vehemently exchanged words back and forth during this semi-heated exchange. He only chimed in when things appeared to be getting a little too out of hand. Because friends, family, partners, or not, blows would begin to fly if things were not properly managed amongst them, as they had done numerous other times before.

That day, Preston didn't feel like breaking up a scuffle or becoming part of one either, especially since Taylor was all that Preston could think about at the moment. He briefly smirked at the thought of her.

Preston calmly placed a hand on the shoulders of the individuals who were displaying the most aggression, trying to bring a sense of calm back within the group, like only he could. He needed to hear as many details as possible from each man's perspective in order to give his most accurate sense of judgment on the issue, or issues at hand. While showing no partiality of any kind.

Preston paused for a brief moment after carefully listening to everything that both men had to say about the matter. He took his time to thoroughly analyze all of the details from different perspectives, with precision and concern due to the severity of the problem.

Preston consulted with his Heavenly Father one last time. He finished up his prayer and grinned. God had once again delivered the perfect answer for him, and he truly loved it. In the calmest tone he could muster, Preston made direct eye contact with each individual who was present before relaying the message. He left each of them flabbergasted with the outcome as he simply quoted the perfect Bible scripture to them without either of them ever acknowledging it in the least.

Each man quietly pondered over his words carefully, then peacefully shook hands and gave one another a brotherly hug.

They walked away together in the same fashion as they had come, while still vaguely debating with one another the whole time that they strolled. That's just who they were. Especially Lil Gary and Bay. Preston laughed.

Lil Gary and Bay blamed the entire disagreement between the group of friends solely on Mystique, saying he had instigated the entire argument just to get a laugh.

Mystique shook his head in disbelief after watching his friend once again solve yet another quarrel amongst men without it leading to any type of physical altercation or bloodshed. Although he witnessed these types of situations constantly being resolved by Preston time and time again, Mystique's amazement always increased every single time.

That was exactly how his best friend had honorably attained the popularized moniker of "Sol." A name that Preston was not only commonly known by throughout the inner-city streets of Nashville, but also within certain Nashville police precincts now as well.

Solely piquing the prime interest of the incredibly beautiful and distinguishably dignified, much older woman, Jezebel La 'Fleur, Taylor's mom.

Chapter 12

Jezebel La'Fleur was an extremely attractive woman with a razor-sharp mind and an even sharper mouthpiece. Two major attributes that definitely came in handy for her while growing up in the ghetto.

The beginning of Jezebel's life was extremely rough on her because the hood took no captives and spared no one. Not even the most beautiful ones.

At the time, Jezebel had two options: get in where she fit in or be swallowed alive by the predators of her community. Becoming somebody's victim or physical plaything for however long that they decided to have their way with her was never going to be a part of her fate. She had a plan, and that was never in her plans.

Not only did Jezebel learn the rules of engagement, but she mastered them quickly in order to survive.

From an early age, Jezebel kept her eyes and ears open to the streets. She listened, and she watched for any and everything out of the ordinary at all times because her life depended on it.

There was always a sense of urgency for Jezebel to be prepared, and not to attempt to get prepared. Her mother had taught her that years ago. And from that moment forward, that's exactly how she always stayed. Focused and Ready!

Ready for trouble, ready for war, and always focused on new opportunities that could change her life's circumstances.

She proudly prided herself on all of the many skills and talents that she'd acquired over the years. Being able to manipulate almost any man of her choosing was at the top of her list. Which Jezebel almost always successfully accomplished, often with nothing more than flashing a smile.

Not to mention her charming personality. Once she exposed that part of herself to them, it was most definitely a wrap. Jezebel arrogantly took pride in that ability.

Jezebel smiled, exposing a perfectly arrayed set of crystal white teeth as she seductively grinned while meticulously scribbling her name in perfect penmanship.

Jezebel La'Fleur.

La'Fleur wasn't actually Jezebel's original last name. But you wouldn't have known that unless you grew up with her and her family in the hellacious living quarters of West Nashville.

Even then, she had somehow fooled quite a few people with this bogus name change. She swore that she and her relatives were of Creole descent. Which was the furthest thing from the truth. But judging from their outer appearances, you could see why so many people had believed it.

Jezebel was mixed with something, but it surely wasn't Creole, unless Creole meant scandalous, conniving, deceptive, dishonest, or just outright selfish. Which is exactly everything that Jezebel appeared to be from birth. Maybe even while in the womb, if you ever had the privilege of actually listening to any of her mother's stories. According to Jezebel's mother, some would say that she was considered to be nothing less than a hellraiser even then.

She caused a pain within the depths of her poor mother's womb that was so severe that she'd physically prayed for death on several occasions, only to be denied, of course.

And from that point forward, Jezebel spared not a single solitary soul from her vindictive ways. Especially not a man. Because to her, they were always the easiest to lead astray.

She laughed at the mere thought of her past buffoonery dealing with men as she fondled the stiffness of her young lover's missile. She disgustedly discarded him from her hand altogether and aggressively told him to leave her sight.

Jezebel menacingly watched her young lover as he confusedly stared back at her for a brief moment. She then shuffled him away like the saddened little puppy he was. She wanted him to give her some type of resistance so that the bipolar part of her brain could be somewhat appeased. Even if it was just a little bit. But still, nothing came.

His lack of a reaction pissed her off even more for no apparent reason at all. It only managed to deepen her scowl to the fourth degree, furthermore, solidifying her previous depiction of what she believed about men within her warped little thought process as an absolute truth, she smiled.

The affair with Jezebel's young lover had been extremely fun and exhilarating for her at first. But it had run its course. Just as all the many other rendezvous, or sexual escapades, that she'd delved into numerous times before.

In her mind, the cat no longer wanted to play with the mouse, and because of that, Jezebel was becoming exceptionally bored with the entire ordeal. So for her, that only meant one of two things: kill him or just let him go.

And as bad as she was leaning towards option number one, she begrudgingly decided against it, only due to the recent demise of her late husband, Mark, of course.

Because if anyone ever discovered what truly happened and why, Jezebel knew for a fact that she would be spending the rest of her natural life behind bars, if not worse.

So that secret she intended to take to the grave!

Chapter 13

Jezebel hadn't seen her children in weeks. She showed the least bit of interest in seeing them. She was having entirely too much fun with her newfound freedom to allow anything or anyone to stand in her way. Especially not some snotty-nosed, begging, and extremely unappreciative kids.

So what if they were her children? Jezebel had never wanted kids of her own from the start, something she openly admitted.

Even now, the thought of being a mother turned her stomach, although each of them was pretty much grown now. Her face twisted in disgust.

Jezebel cringed behind the real reason why she decided to give birth to either of her children in the first place. The truth of the matter is, they were never supposed to be a part of the equation.

Jezebel was a liar amongst liars, and a schemer amongst schemers, from the most deep-seated parts of her demented soul. She became ten times worse as an adult. But one lie had caught up with her in the worst of ways, which still plagued her every single day of her life.

Scowling even deeper, while her nose repeatedly flared up like a raging bull, she reflected back to certain incidents from her past, wishing that she could obliterate every last one of them with just a simple snap of her fingers. Especially the ones that were pertaining to Mark, she grimaced.

Upon meeting Mark, Jezebel had already conjured up a solidified plan to trap him. She knew that he was a bona fide hustler who was clocking major figures in the streets, which was all it took to spark her interest.

So the games began.

Jezebel is what most older women define as the epitome of the word "Gold Digger!" She vowed that Mark was surely going to be her next victim. But Jezebel knew that wasn't going to be an easy task for her to accomplish.

She was going to have to get creative on this one and pull out all of her major tricks to draw Mark into her perfectly woven basket full of deceitful lies. She was willing to do that ten times over, especially when involving money.

Mark wasn't your ordinary, everyday, common street hustler. He was also a businessman. A man whose intellect ranged much higher than most college professors, and whose high IQ scores considered him to be a genius. Making things that much simpler for him when it came to attaining massive amounts of dividends and success from every possible level, while indulging in the streets.

In the beginning, the relationship between Mark and Jezebel started extremely slowly for Jezebel. But when she finally broke through all of Mark's arduous barriers of defense, like the Isley Brothers' famous song, Jezebel knew that it was nothing but smooth sailing from that point forward.

And boy was she right!

Mark wasn't a very trusting man at all. He had been through things and done certain things that most people couldn't possibly come back from. But once you were inside his circle of most trusted individuals, most would say your life was set.

Loyalty meant everything to Mark. It was also one of the main reasons why he had stayed on top in the game for so long. Or at least until he finally decided to call it quits before smoothly making his exit from the game altogether. He understood firsthand that all great things must eventually come to an end.

Mark just didn't want to be sitting in somebody's prison cell, or worse, lying in somebody's cemetery when it actually happened.

The game had been exceptionally good to Mark over the years. So much so that he was now completely leaving it behind and disposing of all scales, beakers, and paraphernalia to never again sell another illegal product for as long as he lived. And for him, that felt amazing.

Jezebel remembered everything as if it were yesterday when she had first lied to Mark about miscarrying their first so-called child. Knowing darn well that she had never truly been pregnant to begin with.

The hurtful look that masked Mark's face in the moment would've been crushing to the common person's spirit. Especially to a mother. But for Jezebel, it meant absolutely nothing at all. Seeing his reaction, she quickly distracted herself to keep from laughing in Mark's face.

Jezebel was heartless. Extremely heartless. She was known as a woman who was born without a soul. And if you examined her or stayed in her presence long enough, you would begin to see it in the callousness of her naturally beautiful, but extremely darkened eyes. Even when she smiled.

Jezebel loved playing games with Mark. She loved tormenting him and causing him to become more perplexed with the entire situation. In that moment, it allowed her to get whatever it was that she wanted from him, money and gifts. And he gave it with no problem.

Mark continuously prayed to God for forgiveness. Figuring that they were going through losing a child due to the dirt that he'd gotten away with while in the streets. He repeatedly repented more and more and prayed harder and harder multiple times a day.

"Lord, please forgive me for I have constantly sinned against You almost every single day of my life, all in the name of trying to make a dollar to feed me and my family. And although I'm not worthy of your mercy, it seems, Lord, please stop allowing our babies to perish because of my sinful ways or past endeavors. Lord, please!" Mark sincerely pleaded, praying to God.

He meant every single word of what he'd professed to God. He prayed with tears flowing from his eyes, dropping his head in defeat. He wondered if God actually listened to sinners such as himself. All the while, truthfully hoping in his heart that He did.

Nothing happened for a while after Mark's prayer, and Jezebel knew exactly why. For the longest time, she'd been sneaking to take birth control pills that were secretly concealed in a vitamin bottle to prevent herself from ever becoming pregnant after she and Mark stopped using protection during intercourse.

Although this would be considered cruel, or just outright deceptive by others, Jezebel didn't give two hoots about what other people cared or thought about it at all. That is, until she had actually gotten pregnant with their very first child. After giving birth to the first child, two more children were born shortly afterwards. All girls!

All the years Jezebel had been lying, playing, and continuously making a fool out of Mark about her so-called pregnancies had finally come back to haunt her. And no matter how slick or deceptive she deemed herself to be at the time, it was more than obvious that she was physically no match for God. She became angry with God, blaming Him for ruining her plans. She was still very upset with Him several years later for what she calls ruining her scheme.

She became so angry that she resented Mark and her very own children with a disdain that was so deeply rooted within her nervous system that it instantly spiked her blood pressure levels to the maximum peak from just a simple thought. Especially Taylor, who was her late husband's true pride and joy. The apple of his no-good eye. And also his identical twin. *"May he rest in piss,"* Jezebel muttered to herself.

She was smiling from ear to ear after visualizing her previous thoughts of Mark actually coming to pass as she checked herself out in the rearview mirror of her brand-new sedan, seductively eyeing the extremely handsome young fellow by the name of Preston, aka "Young Sol."

Chapter 14

Preston was exactly what most women referred to as a bona fide "ladies' man." Not because of promiscuity or physical prowess, but because of the sheer number of beautiful women who constantly pursued him, openly showing him attention and trying to lure him into their beds. These women ranged in age from young to older admirers.

Not underage, of course, but still younger, as in the same age or slightly older. Either way, it didn't matter.

Preston wasn't someone who could be easily swayed or enticed by such simplicity, no matter how attractive someone believed themselves to be. And time and again, he had proven this to be true.

He loved beautiful women, especially Black women. To him, there was nothing more beautiful than the Black woman. But the respect he held for himself and for them outweighed all of that even more.

This was something that he'd specifically become privy to through the constant reading of his Bible, amongst many other Black History books during his time of incarceration.

The knowledge he gained from such information opened Preston's mind tremendously. Retrieving this type of knowledge of self only intrigued him even more, rearranging his entire outlook and depiction of the word "beautiful" altogether. "Beautiful" for him had become something exceedingly much greater than just that of a woman's outer appearance or physical attributes, the typical parts of a female's anatomy that most men so fondly lusted over. Most never fully realize that neither of those assets could ever really begin to compare to the true essence of a Black woman's femininity. Preston disappointingly shook his head at that thought.

Preston knew he was wise beyond his years of existence here on God's green earth. Thanks in large part to the incredible men and women who raised him. They were strong. They were proud. And they were breathtakingly beautiful. Just like many different hues of their deeply enriched skin tones. Especially the women of Preston's family.

His female relatives, neighborhood aunties, and surrogate grandmothers had always made the best out of every possible situation. Like only they could do. But you had to be from some immensely impoverished or extremely humbling beginnings to fully comprehend any of what he was referring to.

With not enough food in the house and their families on the brink of starving, these incredible women somehow always made a way out of no way. Most of the time, taking the smallest amount of rations and surprisingly stretching those meals until every stomach within the household was filled.

Something like when Jesus took the five barley loaves of bread and two single fish in the New Testament of the Bible and fed thousands upon thousands of people. Five thousand to be exact. And because of that, you could always hear their daily praise and gratitude, no matter how tumultuous certain periods of their lives had become, at the time. Because that's just who God created the Black woman to be.

True nurturers. True conquerors. And most of all, True survivors! Preston proudly thought.

There was no other person on Earth who had experienced pain, torment, torture, tragedy, rape, disappointment, or heartache like the Black woman.

Other than the Black man, of course.

And it is because of her, the Black woman, that as a race, they were still able to hold it all together, even still to this very day. Just as she had also done for most Caucasian families back in the day as well. But that's a story that society will forever deny or make small for as long as life exists on God's great earth.

Even though many of these distinguishingly amazing Black women were no longer living, Preston would never forget any of the lessons that were left behind on their behalf. These were characteristics that he would someday be looking for in his future companion when that time presented itself.

Which could be happening a lot sooner than expected, he thought.

He wasn't able to clear his mind of Taylor, the one person who Preston's natural born instincts were telling him, although still pretty much a teenager, already possessed every last one of these incredibly great female qualities.

And soon enough, he would overtly understand exactly why!

Chapter 15

The neighborhood barbecue was in full swing, and everyone seemed to be enjoying all of the festivities. Kids were everywhere, running, laughing, playing, and chasing one another throughout the large vicinity. Most of the adults sat back watching all of the happiness unfold right before their very eyes.

Most would agree that the smell of barbecue always tends to bring people together. Card games, such as spades, bid whist, tonk, rummy, and deuces, brought about some of the most genuine bouts of laughter that many of them had not experienced in quite a while. With brief spats of bickering and a few small arguments closely following suit due to certain individuals who were trying to be slick, which was pretty much almost always the exact same three or four people that it always had been. Even this had become extremely funny to them as well. Especially when all the jokes began to fly. The jokes being thrown normally left all of the accused cheaters somewhat slightly simmering for a brief moment or two before they finally burst into laughter themselves.

But they still never admitted to the cheating, because for them, that was totally against all of the neighborhood slickers' cardinal rule.

Preston loved these types of moments. He loved sitting amongst his people and listening to them tell stories about how it used to be back in the days, while comparing back then to the present. He would listen regardless of how many times he had heard certain stories being told. He was always intrigued.

The elders of Preston's community had struggled to make it through some very tumultuous times. Times that had taken the lives of hundreds of millions of Black men, women, and children, all in the name of racism, bigotry, or just flat-out hatred. Topics that no one ever really wanted to talk about or discuss anymore, except for Black folks. But at the time, what could they possibly do?

Listening attentively, Preston thought, *what could they actually do even now?*

Words such as learn, earn, teach, pray, fight, and excel all simultaneously popped into his spirit in an aggressive nature, because that's exactly what he had been taught to do from the very beginning of his life.

Preston studied the faces that surrounded him and smiled one of the biggest smiles that he'd ever smiled in his entire life. He silently honored all of the incredible men and women who had come before him. Because without them, there would most definitely be no him, and for that, he praised them.

Preston was hysterically laughing as Shaky Jake and old school Paul Bennett openly traded jokes with one another until the linings of people's stomachs were severed as they continuously laughed, gasping for air. Deana, T Hyde, and Shanita all screamed in unison, "Stop y'all stop! I'm about to piss on myself, you fools!"

Cat Bill, Effie, and Kay physically fell to the ground laughing, flaring their hands and arms up in surrender, while struggling to breathe.

Moments like these were priceless. And so were the people of Preston's community. Every single ghetto in America was filled with your Shaky Jake's, Big Nose Ark's, William McDowell's, Ha's Ha's, and Gene Ewing's. They were extremely funny and talented individuals who could make some of the absolute worst times and abhorred living conditions, not only hilarious, but extremely viable as well.

Sadly enough, almost none of these exceedingly gifted, talented, or profoundly creative individuals would ever get the opportunity to share any of their amazing gifts with the world. Mostly due to the pigmentation of their skin, and their lack of resources, finances, or simply just because of where they were from.

Pain masked Preston's face for a brief second, but he quickly pushed it aside and proudly kept smiling and laughing as he observed all of the many "Hood Superstars" that surrounded him. Because to him and so many others, that's exactly who they were, whether they realized it or not.

Preston suddenly shifted his undivided attention towards the beautiful being, Taylor, making her way down Indiana Avenue, walking alongside several of her family members. Preston cooly grinned, vowing to himself that he would at least spark up some type of conversation with the mean-spirited young lady. Even if it physically embarrassed him. Something told him that Taylor was more than well worth it.

Chapter 16

Taylor was very observant of her surroundings. And though it was a tad bit uncomfortable for her at first, she absolutely loved everything about what she was seeing. She wasn't what one would consider to be "green or naïve," but she had definitely been somewhat sheltered from certain lifestyles and environments.

Mainly due to her mother. After her mother escaped the so-called "hood," for better words, she never wanted to set foot back into that abhorrently decrepit part of her past ever again, and therefore never allowed her children to either. Or at least that's how she had always explained it to Taylor and her siblings, and how Taylor vividly remembered.

Taylor was definitely her father's child, and it physically showed in more ways than one. Especially now, more than ever. What she was seeing and experiencing was nothing less than pure, unadulterated beauty at its finest. Something that could never formally be put into words from her perspective, even if she artistically tried.

Taylor had never seen so many beautiful Black faces gathered together having so much fun in her entire life, and she admired that. Her father would always tell her these amazing stories about where and how he had grown up, or about all of the love and camaraderie that existed within the so-called "hood," time and time again. But physically seeing it for herself firsthand was something entirely different altogether.

Astoundingly breathtaking, if trying to sum it all up with just a few simple words. And completely different from what she had ever heard about or physically witnessed on any of her local Nashville news stations, which more than always painted most of the Black communities as extremely negative, while the majority of those very same types of crimes or incidents were happening across the tracks in the so-called "white" suburban neighborhoods of America as well.

Drug usage, drug sales, and common acts of "white-on-white" violence were just as normal there as it was in the "hood." But these were not topics that one would openly hear being discussed out in public places or in the downtown legislature buildings abroad, like they frequently were when pertaining to Blacks.

Taylor shook her head in disappointment at this sad truth. She thought of her father, reminiscing about all of the incredible times they had spent together, talking and laughing with one another. Or how he would always take Taylor and her siblings over to their GiGi's house just to check on older relatives and a few family friends.

Taylor's father always expressed that checking on family was a necessity. It was something he needed to do to be reminded exactly what true love looked and felt like firsthand, because the house that Mark built with Jezebel never exuded any of those specific family-like qualities at all. This was the exact reason why Taylor had come to her GiGi's home after his passing.

Taylor needed to experience, feel, and visualize what true love looked and felt like once again. And her father's side of the family would be that for her and much more. This she factually knew.

So there she was, finally far away from all of her mother's scrutiny, judgment, jealousy, and mistreatment. Taylor had no intentions of ever returning to her mother's way of life, if she could help it.

Pain pierced her heart as she thought about her father and sisters, but Taylor didn't cry this time. Instead, she smiled at all of the beautiful people who encompassed her now. She smiled at all the genuine love that was being displayed amongst everyone within the area. But most importantly, Taylor was smiling due to the handsome young man, Preston, who confidently intruded upon her personal space.

And for some odd reason, Taylor didn't resist or put up much of a fuss this time about anything at all. Instead, she merely went with the flow of things and pleasantly enjoyed the perfectly aligned smile of the stranger that everyone called "Preston." He respectfully reached for Taylor's hand to formally introduce himself.

She was smiling even harder now, while somewhat trying to control her nerves, because his touch felt amazing. So she allowed it.

Taylor's heartbeat suddenly quickened, and she couldn't explain what was happening. She stared up into Preston's slanted brown eyes as she continued holding onto his hand. And it was in that moment that Taylor began to feel something that she had never before felt with any other man than that of her very own father. Love. The why was puzzling to Taylor, but the feeling was a sense of security.

Chapter 17

Preston's touch disarmed Taylor's toughness, causing it to instantly dissipate, exposing her to an unfamiliar vulnerability deeply within herself that had never been tapped into before. Surprisingly enough, she liked it. But what she couldn't manage to understand was the sudden sense of security that she felt while in the presence of this stranger, Preston. And that Taylor did not like one bit. Or so she tried to believe.

Taylor battled with the mixed emotions that were wavering within her spirit without her permission, while desperately trying to maintain her composure. But the sudden butterflies dancing within the pit of her stomach had her feeling giddy inside, and all she could do at the time was relent. Taylor skeptically enjoyed everything about the young man standing before her.

There was nothing special about Preston's introduction to Taylor, yet still, his voice sent shockwaves to the depths of her inner core, something she could not deny. Taylor thought Preston's voice was just as cool and as smooth as his stroll.

Taylor tried to keep her poker face intact as she fought against the nagging emotions dwelling inside her, internally smiling big. She couldn't fathom allowing this stranger to witness any of the inner thoughts or feelings that she was dealing with at the moment. But her feelings were becoming harder for her to disguise.

Taylor glanced up at Preston as her eyes traveled from his face to her hand for what appeared to be several seconds, as some of those emotions reverberated throughout her entire body from head to toe. But she had a little bit more self-control over her outward feelings, other than what she was feeling on the inside. Taylor managed to calmly speak, shocking Preston as she clearly verbalized every syllable of her sentence with much precision.

"Is this what you do to all of the new young ladies that just so happen to cross your path, ummm Preston, is it?" Taylor feigned not to remember his name before continuing. "Rudely take people's hands captive while holding it against their will. Even after you've made your so-called introduction. Well, if so, then I truly suggest for you to work on your manners, young man, because such behavior is absolutely prohibited by my family. And the punishment for such penalties could possibly result in death!"

Taylor emphatically emphasized her words, making sure her tone had just the right amount of spunk in it for Preston to fully understand that she was dead serious. But yet, enough softness for him to acknowledge that she sorta didn't mind.

Preston smiled his coolest smile before attempting to answer, pausing for a brief second or two before responding. Something that he'd religiously learned to do many years back, especially during the many unsuccessful interrogations that he'd previously undergone. Because for him, it was always imperative that he made the appropriate statement at all times. Even when it couldn't land him back in jail.

Preston smirked. He knew that words were powerful. Extremely powerful. And this, Preston fully understood firsthand. He had always made it his business to think before he ever reacted or spoke. As the Bible clearly states in Proverbs 18:21, "Death and Life were in the power of the tongue." And although still very much a young man, Preston had already witnessed and experienced just how powerful the tongue could truly be. Especially when pertaining to death.

So, with that being said, Preston smoothly pulled Taylor closer to him and softly whispered into her ear, instantly plastering a huge smile upon her beautiful face. His mouth close to her ear further heightened the joy of her already amazing day. But the world nor anyone else around them would know what those words were, because whatever it was that Preston had said to Taylor during that time was specifically for her ears only.

Taylor pleasantly smiled at Preston's remarks as his words slowly began chipping away at her once extremely hardened exterior. And just when he thought that he was finally breaking the ice with her, Taylor's demeanor once again became exceptionally cold and clammy. She suddenly retracted her hand from Preston's grasp and instantly recoiled her entire body as if she'd just seen a ghost.

"Momma!" Taylor surprisingly hissed.

Taylor watched as the woman who had birthed her but had never really been much of a parent to her at all walked closer to where she stood. Jezebel slowly made her way towards Taylor and Preston with one of the phoniest smiles that Taylor had ever witnessed on any human being. And with that thought in mind, Taylor realized that everything was about to go from great to extremely worst for her in the blink of an eye. Especially when her mother abruptly stopped in front of them to speak.

"Hello, daughter. Now, who is this extremely handsome and enchantingly stylish young gentleman here, might I ask?" Jezebel incredulously inquired. She seductively winked her eye at Preston while blatantly ignoring her daughter's attempted response. All the while, Jezebel knew exactly who Preston was from the very beginning, as she overbearingly took over Preston and Taylor's entire conversation.

"Run along now, dear. Your presence is no longer needed here anymore, little girl. Oh yeah, and tell your grandmother that I said... well, I don't actually care what you tell her!" Jezebel sarcastically spat with an apparent hint of venom dripping from her remark.

She looped her arm into Preston's and walked away from Taylor, disrespectfully pulling him from Taylor's presence. Preston, confused, looked back in Taylor's direction in pure astonishment.

Chapter 18

As Preston and Jezebel walked away arm in arm, fumes seethed from Taylor's scalp like heat rays rising off the streets of Las Vegas strip on a hot summer day.

The audacity of her mother embarrassing her that way in front of all those people. Especially in front of Preston, she thought with a menacing scowl, glowering at her mother even more profusely as she watched Jezebel flirtatiously staring up into Preston's eyes while repeatedly caressing certain parts of his chiseled frame.

Completely taken aback by Jezebel's behavior, Preston respectfully voiced his opinion about it once out of earshot of Taylor or any other person who had just witnessed what had taken place.

He looked back at Taylor, noticing the pain and anger in her face. He somehow felt partially responsible for assisting in her hurt. Seeing her in pain was making it that much easier for Preston to say everything that he was about to say to Jezebel in that moment if he didn't figure out a way to calm himself down first.

Preston was livid. And it took everything within him not to physically snap at the much older woman who stood before him. He took several deep breaths in hopes of recapturing his composure. Because the person that was staring back at him was definitely the devil reincarnated, Preston acknowledged.

And just like in the famous movie title, Jezebel was also wearing "Prada."

Preston had seen Satan manifest in many different types of individuals while growing up in the ghetto. But never had he witnessed Satan use someone as beautiful or as well put together as Mrs. Jezebel La'Fleur.

Or had he…

At one point, Satan himself was considered as being extremely handsome and very talented, some would say. Especially when pertaining to music. Preston instantly rehashed certain books from the Bible that he'd read several times over during his time of incarceration, like Isaiah and Ezekiel, which pretty much helped sum up almost every fact that he was thinking about at the time.

What Preston was currently observing from Jezebel at that moment, he honestly hadn't witnessed since the incident had transpired between him, Mystique, and the perpetrator who had tragically lost his life several years prior.

And to be truthful about it, it kinda spooked him, mentally sending Preston back to a place in time that he never wanted to relive ever again. But yet and still, there it was… Evil!

Pure unadulterated evil, as a matter of fact!

But this time around, that evil appeared to be more than a hundred times worse. Preston had once been told that the eyes never lied. And neither did his gut instincts, for that matter.

Preston fully understood that if he wasn't extremely careful while dealing with this much older, but immensely ravishing individual that was standing before him confidently, brandishing her signature smile of death, that he and Taylor's lives could both possibly be in danger at any given moment.

Because hell hath no fury like a woman scorned, it was stated.

And Preston wholeheartedly believed that Jezebel La'Fleur was a true testament of that very fact. This he could also sense.

Chapter 19

"Ugggh!!! GiGi, why is she even here?" Taylor frustratingly expressed a tad bit too loudly for GiGi's liking.

GiGi gave Taylor a look, quickly calming her granddaughter down with nothing more than a simple glare.

Taylor instantaneously caught her grandmother's drift and suddenly shifted her entire attitude in record time. She knew that Mrs. Jackie Marie didn't play.

The look that GiGi had given Taylor silently spoke volumes without ever making a sound. "Because wherever you acted out, was exactly where you got knocked out," was GiGi's famous motto. And she truthfully meant that with all her heart.

GiGi didn't care if you were at church, in the grocery store check-out line, or even inside of the police station. For her, none of that mattered at all. If you were wrong, then you most definitely got busted on with no hesitation. And that's just how it was.

Not only had Taylor recaptured her composure, she also intently listened to her GiGi as she began to speak, respectfully maintaining eye contact the whole time as she continuously dropped her jewels.

GiGi skillfully gathered her thoughts, being exceptionally careful not to say the wrong things to her grandchild. Because after all, Jezebel was still Taylor's mother, whether she acted like one or not. GiGi finally formulated her sentences in the best way that she could without being overly offensive.

"Grandbaby, don't let your mother ruin this moment for you, darling. Because it appears that that's exactly what she's trying to do right now. Why is she here? That I do not know. But I'm pretty sure that it's not with good intentions. So please always keep that in mind, ok. I've never really condoned your mother's actions at all. But your father loved her for some odd reason, so I tolerated it for the sake of his happiness. Plus, I had to remain extremely close in order to watch over you and your sisters as much as I could," GiGi stated.

"Because some of the things that I heard and witnessed firsthand at certain points, should I say, were somewhat unfitting for a mother to do. And that I could not tolerate, so at times I would get involved. But only when pertaining to the well-being of you and your sisters. Which Jezebel never liked one bit," GiGi concluded.

GiGi led Taylor in the opposite direction of her mother in order to escape her presence. As they walked, she introduced her to more people in the neighborhood. They stopped to fraternize with Mrs. Maxine, who just so happened to be her grandmother's closest friend.

Taylor genuinely smiled as she observed the much older women cackle and interact with one another. It was sort of like watching a television sitcom in a sense. They were both extremely funny, loud, and very adorable. But also a tad bit nosy. They talked about any and everything under the sun, including people, as if they hadn't seen or heard from each other in years, knowing that they'd just gotten off the phone with one another moments prior. But yet again, here they were.

Taylor laughed at the women while greeting several other people along the way. She was getting more acquainted with some of her father's oldest neighborhood friends. They shared story after story with her about a lot of their past endeavors together, which she definitely loved. She soaked up every detail like a sponge as they rambled along.

"Taylor, your father this... Taylor, your father that!" She repeatedly heard with so much passion. They laughed and joked while filling her in on so many new things about her dad. Taylor swore that she could actually feel her father's presence amongst them, which was probably true.

She enjoyed her father's friends, and boy did he have a lot of them. People who, in turn, also seemed to have loved and cared for him just as much as she did. This made Taylor smile.

Even in her father's absence, Mark was still finding ways to not only bring enjoyment into his daughter's life but also security. And she knew this had come to pass for her through her GiGi and several of his closest friends.

As she looked up towards the heavens, where she knew her father resided, she solemnly thanked God for the incredible man that she would forever remember as "Dad." And for so many others, as "friend."

No matter how much time had passed, Taylor proudly gleamed.

"Thank you for this day, Lord. Thank you also for blessing me with the best father that a little girl could ever possibly have as well," Taylor happily expressed towards the heavens.

"Although I truly miss him, Lord, I know that he's currently in good hands, because Your will is perfect. So I have no more worries at all on my father's behalf. But if I'm worthy, I would like to ask You one simple favor for myself, when, and if that time comes for me. And that is, to please bless me with someone that's just as amazing as my father was, when it's finally my time to marry. In Jesus name." Taylor boldly professed and made clear.

She started reminiscing about Preston's touch once again and how incredible it had made her feel inside. She carefully scanned the so-called "Big Field" one last time in hopes of locating his handsome face, but did not. She wondered if she actually ever would again, or if her mom had also taken him away from her as well, just as she'd done with her father. Taylor seriously questioned as her resentment once again began to resurface.

Chapter 20

Jezebel noticed the obvious attraction that existed between Preston and Taylor. But daughter or not, she would not be denied. The mere existence of her daughter's attraction to Preston only intrigued her more.

A blinding jealousy encompassed Jezebel's entire body from head to toe. Especially when she saw the skepticism in Preston's eyes as he caringly looked back in Taylor's direction.

Jezebel was not going to allow this to happen to her again. She seriously contemplated the situation as a vision of her deceased husband, and Taylor vividly replayed in her mind. The laughing, joking, and playing around with one another for the thousandth time. The reminder of their perfect relationship pissed Jezebel off even more. She attempted to annihilate those unwarranted memories from her thoughts altogether.

Jezebel thought that Mark should have been with her the majority of the time, instead of with their children. She had no regrets about her selfish ways, even though they were her children; that's exactly the way she felt. The thought caused her to clench her teeth in anger while unsuccessfully trying to maintain her sanity. She vowed to spit on Mark's grave. Jezebel verbally cursed Mark once again in her mind as if he were still amongst the living. All the while, she hoped that Preston couldn't sense the sudden change in her demeanor as she desperately tried her best to conjure up a smile. But she failed. She slowly counted backward from a hundred in hopes of minimizing her rage.

Jezebel was tired of always having to compete with her children. Especially Taylor.

And this time she swore not to lose!

Not without capitalizing on it first.

But what was there really to gain or benefit from this aimless debacle? She wanted nothing more than to see her daughter's feelings crushed once again. This was something Jezebel cherished, yet also vaguely abhorred in a sick type of way. This is how it was when it pertained to her happiness.

As Jezebel has said before, she never really wanted kids in the first place! She reiterated that statement to herself once again as she wickedly grinned.

She thought back to the days when she was a child. Jezebel La'Fleur was created out of pain and suffering and brought into this world to live in pain and suffering. She had also given her poor little mother nothing but pain and suffering during her entire pregnancy and beyond. So it was fair to say that Jezebel only understood pain and suffering firsthand. Pain that she naturally inflicted upon every living being that had crossed her path from the day that she was born.

Especially her husband and kids. It was a known fact that those closest to you almost always got the worst end of the stick, as older black folks would say. Mark and Taylor were the closest to her, and in this case, that statement proved to be factually true.

Anger seethed from Jezebel's pores as she continuously revisited parts of her past involving Mark and Taylor. Two people that Jezebel had once cherished and admired so much at one point that she eventually began to hate them. Hated them solely because they knew how to love someone other than themselves and love them correctly, genuinely. Something that Jezebel obviously just didn't know how to do or attempt to do if she tried.

Tears formed in Jezebel's eyes, but her lack of emotions refused to allow them to fall. She blinked, putting them back into their proper place. A place far away that had no bearing within her soul anymore, something Jezebel believed made a person weak!

Weaknesses eventually made you vulnerable, and vulnerabilities sometimes tended to get you hurt or killed! Those were words that someone extremely close to her, at one point in time, surely loved to quote. That is, until several of those same weaknesses they so adamantly spoke about, in regard to actually protecting themselves, had eventually come back to destroy them years later. And Jezebel had witnessed every single moment of it firsthand.

Jezebel gloated because she was the main one responsible for their demise. She evilly smirked, seductively rubbing her hand over Preston's forearm once again while vowing for him to be next.

Especially now that she realized that Preston truly adored Taylor, and from her observations, Taylor was very much smitten with him as well.

Chapter 21

Taylor had voluntarily traveled to and from the grocery store on several different occasions, hoping to catch another glimpse of Preston's face. But each time, she had no luck in locating him. It was starting to be frustrating for her, to say the least.

Taylor was still a little salty with her mother for ruining their conversation several days earlier and had been trying her best to let it all go. But it was unpleasant thoughts of her mom, and moments such as these, that made it impossible for her to forgive.

Taylor had been raised to respect her parents and elders, regardless of the situation, which was sometimes a major challenge for her. Especially when it came to her mother. But somehow, she always managed to do the right thing, though she didn't fully understand how. She just attributed it all to God, something she openly acknowledged.

Taylor walked back to GiGi's house from the store with both hands full of groceries when one of the bags slowly started to slip from her grasp. She held on as tightly as she could. She desperately tried regaining her grip, but it was too late. The contents spilled onto the pavement, shattering certain items into what seemed to be a thousand pieces, causing her to swear.

Not too loudly, but loud enough for a few onlookers to hear her frustrating rants, with Preston being amongst the few.

"Wow! What a foul mouth we have on such a beautiful day, Young Lady. Does your grandmother know that you use such vulgarity out in public? If not, then I really think that she should. Because to be honest with you, your mouth is absolutely terrible." Preston stated while disguising his voice. He made sure to keep his identity concealed as he watched Taylor from behind as she pointlessly tried to savor whatever items she could.

Taylor desperately tried to refrain from cursing for a second time. Which only seemed to infuriate her even more. She swallowed as much of her frustration as she could before standing. Taking a few more much-needed deep breaths to further help settle her nerves, before turning to face the antagonist, who to her was obviously not even man enough to help assist with her dilemma. She turned to face him, flabbergasted by who was standing in front of her. Preston.

Preston greeted Taylor with his highly infectious smile, confidently showing off a perfectly aligned set of straight white teeth that looked to have been recently cleaned. He extended a small stack of money in her direction. Money that he wanted to give Taylor to help replace the broken goods. Standing there, extending his arm, he quoted Billy Dee Williams' famous line from the "Lady Sings the Blues" movie. "You want my arm to fall off?" Preston repeated the line just as smoothly, if not smoother, as Billy Dee Williams had. He was looking Taylor directly in her eyes as he spoke.

Still very much seething with anger, Taylor tried her best not to smile but couldn't help it. She still allowed the money to dangle from Preston's fingertips for a moment or two longer before saying a word. "And what is that for?" Taylor incredulously asked, snidely looking at Preston's outstretched hand as if it were some type of plague.

However, she was somewhat impressed by his current act of kindness, but she wasn't about to show it. She remained firmly fixated in her position with bags steadily leaking, creating a mess smack dead in the center of the walkway as if she wasn't the least bit concerned.

"Just a little something to help replace GiGi's items, unless you plan on trying to explain where the rest of her groceries are once you finally get there. And good luck with that, because I'm sure that she gave you more than enough money to cover everything she needed." Preston jokingly stated. He outstretched the money towards Taylor even further this time around.

Taylor playfully but aggressively snatched it from his hand, rolling her eyes while doing so as she secretly smiled.

"Forget you! I'm not clumsy if that's what you're trying to insinuate, Mr. Funny Man! And I will definitely

75

be giving you this money back, too! Just as soon as I get to my GiGi's house, you little Richard Pryor wanna be!" Taylor laughed as Preston humorously shrugged his shoulders, giggling himself.

They both headed back inside the store.

Taylor enjoyed Preston's company as they traveled from aisle to aisle, cracking jokes on one another while gathering items. It was as if they'd known one another for quite a while, instead of a few days. Their behavior surprised them both, seeing that their chemistry was just so natural.

Preston carried all of the bags from the grocery store to GiGi's house as they talked, completely ridding Taylor of her earlier burdens, although she pretty much insisted on helping.

Upon arrival, Taylor held the door open for Preston as he made his way inside. Taylor retrieved the remaining grocery bags that were left on the porch to keep Preston from making a second trip, which he recognized, making him smile. It wasn't much to some, but for Preston, it meant a lot because there had been numerous times where he had lent a helping hand to others, and in return, they had selfishly left him to do all of the work by himself.

With that small and simple gesture, Taylor had earned herself another golden star on Preston's list without her even knowing it. Preston thought to himself that it was something exceedingly special about Taylor. There was a connection that existed amongst them that could not be denied, and Taylor felt the exact same way.

But yet, neither of them could quite figure out exactly what that special thing was, so they both decided to keep it under wraps until it presented itself. If it ever did, Preston and Taylor both privately thought.

Two hours later, Preston checked his watch and stood up to leave. He modestly hugged Taylor and GiGi before heading towards the door. He thanked them for all of the laughs and hospitality as he strolled away.

When he left their home, Preston never once noticed Jezebel or her young ex-lover secretly watching his every move as he smoothly turned the corner, disappearing.

"Hump! So that's Preston, huh? aka "Young Sol?" Shiiiid, he doesn't look so darn clever to me!" Jezebel's jealous-hearted young lover emphatically proclaimed with much seriousness in his tone. "Well, let's see if he has a solution for this?" The young ex-lover arrogantly replied, exposing one of the biggest handguns that Jezebel had ever seen in her entire life. He slowly admired it by twisting it from side to side. He was glad that he'd found who he assumed to be one of the main culprits who had murdered his big cousin Ron.

Jezebel, who was now suddenly turned on by the gun and the aggressiveness of her former young ex-lover's actions, slowly began exposing another one of his hardened members, feverishly placing it inside of her deceitful jaws, literally working her voodoo on the young boy's mental, until his words were no longer coherent.

Chapter 22

Preston and Taylor woke up at almost the exact same time that morning, as if they'd slept together under the same roof, or in the same bed. They both felt refreshed and ready for the world.

The previous day had been nothing short of amazing for them. And to be honest, they were already looking forward to doing it all over again soon. If it were up to Preston, it would be that same day.

Preston smiled at himself in his bedroom mirror as he meticulously double-checked his appearance to make sure that everything was copacetic. While Taylor, who was only a few short blocks away at the time, was in her grandmother's bathroom, unknowingly doing the exact same thing. She struck pose after pose from several different positions, checking herself out from every possible angle before finally making her exit.

Taylor loved what she had seen staring back at her in the mirror. But she would've loved it even more had Preston been hugged up on her from behind. She shyly giggled to herself due to her previous thoughts and truly realized that it was completely out of the norm for her.

But thoughts of Preston and her together felt amazing, so what the heck, Taylor justified.

Taylor thought that although Preston was only a few months older than she was, he carried himself as if he were much older. She figured it was due to all of the things that he'd been through in the streets at such an early age. Things that most people would've never known anything about unless they were close to him, like his best friend Mystique.

Mystique was the one and only person in the whole world that Preston had ever fully come to trust. He shared this with Taylor, with a look of assurance in his eyes, as he confidently spoke his truth. Suddenly releasing an uncomfortable smirk and rubbing his head, while pondering over old memories.

Mystique was more of a brother to Preston than just a friend. Something that was rare amongst people within their community, even when pertaining to family.

Mystique and Preston were two young people who shared a lot of the same core values and principles. They had both grown up during some very tumultuous times due to their extremely impoverished beginnings. And the lack of food, funds, love, and dingy clothing were never really going to be an exception for these almost starving adolescents.

They both had become haphazardly mischievous in a lot of their ways just to attain a meal at least twice a day. Not only for themselves, but for several other family members and friends as well. They sometimes walked miles and miles to many dangerous neighborhoods to pull off most of these felonious capers.

All in the name of survival, of course.

Especially dangerous when pertaining to the white neighborhoods, where merely walking home from school or leaving football, basketball, or wrestling practice without a sizable enough crowd to help fight alongside you during those times could possibly get you severely beaten or killed.

This only solidified their bond with one another even more. There had never been a time, regardless of the dangers or circumstances, that they had ever left each other hanging or unprotected. Even when involving death.

Mystique was like a shadow. He was always quiet, stayed to himself, and remained in the cut. He never divulged much of his thoughts or truthfully conversed with much of anyone. Especially if he didn't know you.

But even when you did know him, depending on who you were, you still wouldn't receive anything more than a head nod or some type of quick gesture that mostly still didn't involve words. Because that's just who he was.

Mystique had watched several so-called friends instantly turn into blatant enemies in the blink of an eye. He never truly allowed anyone to get too close to him or know what he was ever thinking at any time. He wouldn't hesitate to diminish anything or anyone that even remotely posed the least bit of a threat to himself or

Preston. Something that most individuals in the streets fully understood firsthand.

But there would always be those few who refused to accept or acknowledge the true severity of these actions and circumstances. So for them, Mystique was always more than prepared.

With the previous information that Mystique had recently acquired while doing what he does best, which was lurking somewhere deep in the cut, that information he would solemnly keep to himself and never disclose to anyone for the time being.

Not even to his best friend Preston, until it was time to strike. And strike he most definitely would in due time, Mystique thought to himself before fading back into the shadows from whence he'd slightly emerged to avoid being seen.

Chapter 23

The semi-brief encounter of sexual satisfaction that Jezebel performed on her young lover was all the fuel that he needed for her to get exactly what she wanted from him. She didn't even finish what she started, which was the most important part of her plan. She was once again toying with her young lover's head, stringing him along and leaving his testicles full of semen as she began faking another tantrum.

Sexually frustrated, backed-up, angry, and extremely horny, her young lover suddenly became more perplexed when Jezebel stopped performing her insatiable mouth exercises on him. Her actions, or lack of, sent several unrecognizable endorphins coursing through his brain, turning it into what felt like mush.

"This is all you want from me, isn't it?" Jezebel yelled into her young lover's face while forcing tears from her eyes that instantaneously began to flow. "You don't love me! You don't love me at all, do you? All you want to do is use me! Use me for my money and sex! That's it, isn't it! Isn't it!!" Jezebel continually ranted.

Theatrically, she cried, sending even more tears streaming down her cheeks as she drifted more into character. She delivered her last and final statement with much more moxie.

"Well, I'm nobody's fool, young man. Nobody's! Do you understand me!" Jezebel yelled while pointing her finger towards his face. She attempted to slap his cheek, but her young lover quickly caught Jezebel's hand, avoiding her blow. He gripped her hand tightly, allowing her to feel his strength.

His actions turned her on once again, and she instantly climbed his physically fit body as if she were climbing a tree. She didn't stop until his manhood desperately found the entrance of her panty-less womb, where she aggressively slammed herself up and down on his enlarged member like some type of crazed maniac, almost driving the young boy completely insane with every powerful thrust. She seductively whispered her demands. "Kill them! Kill them all for me, baby! Kill them all!" Jezebel manipulatively urged him on.

Her weight slightly shifted in the young boy's arms from the buckling of his knees. He rapidly recovered his footing just before the syncopated explosions pleasurably rushed from each of their bodies in a lustful fashion.

This left both Jezebel and her young lover desperately spent, gasping for air, and staring one another directly in the eyes without speaking a word.

Chapter 24

Several days had passed, and today was the day that Preston and Taylor had finally agreed upon meeting again. Although very much excited about their plans for the day, they still appeared to be a tad bit more nervous than usual.

But the indescribable eeriness that resided within the depths of Preston's gut appeared to be more than six times greater. But he disregarded those feelings altogether and simply blamed what he was feeling on his nerves.

He never once fathomed the thought that an attempt was about to be made upon his life due to the highly problematic schemes and deceitful lies of Mrs. Jezebel La'Fleur. Taylor's very own manipulatively cancerous mother.

Jezebel had withstood all that she could stand when it came to Taylor. And now that she realized just how much her daughter liked and very much admired Preston, Jezebel decided to cause even more pain in her middle child's life by completely snatching her happiness away. Physically doing so, she sadistically thought.

To be blatantly honest about everything, Jezebel was sick and tired of witnessing all the lovey-dovey, stomach-churning antics that both Taylor and Preston were so openly displaying with one another. Jezebel suddenly shuddered with anger, instantly vowing to herself and whomever it was that she served, which wasn't God, to completely bring it all to a crashing halt. And she meant every word.

So there they both were again.

Both Jezebel and her young lover were once again stalking Preston for a second or third time, maybe even more, silently observing the precision of Preston's every move in order to devise their attack on him with much vengeance, tactfully. And rightfully so, Jezebel thought, because she wasn't in the business of being caught, she affirmed.

For this reason, Jezebel was setting the stage up for her "young flunky," I mean, "young lover," to purposely take the fall for everything, if anything were to take place. Because all of the evidence and motives were definitely pointing towards him by all means, and Jezebel was clearly making sure of it.

Jezebel deviously grinned as she decided to once again give her very rambunctious young lover another added boost of confidence to his already overly inflated and highly overzealous ego, by repeatedly reciting some of the exact same words that he'd frequently been telling himself over and over again. But this time she said them in a much more influential way.

She softly and seductively stated, "He doesn't seem so darn smart to me either, baby. Definitely not smarter than you," Jezebel sweetly purred into her young lover's ear just before kissing the spot from which she was now slowly removing her hand as her words slithered from her mouth.

"So get on out there and show these cocksuckers exactly who the hell you are, Daddy! Because it's time to avenge your big cousin Ron's death, so that he may finally rest in peace!" Jezebel concluded as she seductively leaned over him to push open the driver's side door.

She closely observed his every move as the fuel from her extremely toxic pep-talk slowly began to take root within the young man's spirit. Her words deepened the murderous scowl that existed upon his face. Jezebel decided to pour it on just a little bit thicker in that moment in order for him to fully receive the message.

Jezebel assumed that her plan was working out perfectly fine on her behalf as her young lover quickly cocked his weapon and exited the vehicle in a crazed manner. He violently slammed the door behind him and aggressively commanded her to "stay put!"

He once again repeated the same words to himself for the thousandth time, as he rapidly crouched low to the ground to further conceal his identity. "Man, these cocksuckers got me messed up! But they gon' learn today! Because every last one of these fools is about to go meet their Maker!" The young lover angrily spat, haphazardly discharging bullet after bullet from his weapon. When he was done, he scrambled his way back to an empty vehicle, where his car keys visibly rested on the vehicle's floorboard in plain sight, but behind locked doors.

Chapter 25

With panicked-filled eyes, and a heart rate that appeared to be trying to break free from the young man's chest cavity, Jezebel's young lover could acutely hear the rapid palpitation of sudden footsteps drawing closer and closer to him with every fleeting second. He desperately tried to get into the vehicle without having to break out its window. But to no avail, luck wasn't appearing to be on his side in the moment. He began to slightly panic.

"Think!... Think!... Think!" The young lover constantly recited to himself over and over again.

He quickly surveyed his surroundings with rapidly moving eyes, which were performing with the agility of a scanner. His eyes were darting to and fro, backwards and forwards, in search of anything that could help get him out of his current predicament.

But he still came up with nothing to help him in that moment.

And that's when he saw it. A brick!

It was the appropriate size for the job that he had in mind. Maybe even a little bigger than he'd expected after he picked it up. But in either case, he thought, it was certainly gonna have to do the trick because he was running out of time.

He removed his shirt from his body and quickly covered the boulder with its fabric in hopes of somehow lessening the sound of shattering glass. He instinctively released it from his hand and into the passenger-side window with much added force.

You could faintly hear the sound of the breaking glass. Which was good, and everything appeared to be copacetic. He quickly climbed inside the vehicle and grabbed the keys. He instantly fired up the engine and nervously threw it in reverse, making his getaway.

Once he was out of danger, he released a huge sigh of relief. As the coast became clearer, the young lover began to celebrate alone, cheering and chanting loudly in a highly intense fashion while driving down the road.

He was satisfied with what he'd accomplished and felt the least bit of remorse about any of it at all. He was gleefully yelling "Hoorah" as if he were some type of highly decorated soldier who had fought on a battlefield. Or who had just recently been presented with the "Purple Heart" and the "Medal of Honor," for his current acts of so-called bravery. For him, that's exactly what it felt like.

He gloated a little bit more as he began talking to himself. "Man, my big cousin would truly be super proud of me right now, if he were here! But don't trip, big cuz because lil cuz took care of that for you, for real! And it's only the beginning, Ron just watch!" The young lover openly professed, hitting the accelerator a little harder. He was feeling himself as he began regaining his so-called cool, becoming more comfortable with every passing second as he eased the vehicle to a smooth cruise.

Casually bobbing his head to "Never Seen A Man Cry," by the rapper Scarface, he confidently recited every lyric of the song word for word.

"Imagine life at its full peak then imagine lying dead in the arms of your enemy!" The young lover ardently recited the lyrics over and over again, pressing rewind on his CD player to continuously hear that specific verse multiple times. He stopped at Richard's Market to play his numbers with intentions of also grabbing some beer and rolling papers for his weed so that he could extend the celebration.

But what he didn't expect, and never noticed, was the extremely sharpened, cold, hard steel that placed his life into "park," as the engine softly purred like a kitten, quietly idling until his foot finally began mashing the gas.

Chapter 26

The blurred image slid from the vehicle just as quickly as the blade of the knife had easily glided from one end to the other of the young lover's throat. They walked away unnoticed or unidentified by anyone. As the assailant casually rounded the corner of Richard's Market, they quickly disappeared somewhere deep within the darkness, without ever making a sound.

There was no rustling of leaves. No sudden breakage of small sticks or twigs. There was absolutely nothing to detect that someone had ever been present there at all. And it wasn't until some common straggler from the local neighborhood, who was out begging for change in hopes to possibly attain a few loose Kool cigarettes, and maybe even a beer, that the body was accidentally stumbled upon.

The site of the young lover's body was horrifying, causing the individual to fall to the pavement as they desperately scrambled to get away from the vehicle and quickly back onto their feet. But when they tried to stand, they clumsily hit the tarmac for a second time, realizing they had sprained their ankle.

Yelping at the top of their lungs, other onlookers suddenly became a bit more interested in what was going on. Big Richard, of Richard's Market, curiously exited his establishment with a pistol in hand, ready for whatever as he instinctively eased the hammer back on his weapon.

Richard's eyes slowly followed the astonished stares from all the other patrons who were occupying his parking lot. But nothing could prepare him for the gruesome scene that he was about to witness. His eyes landed on the traumatic sight of the victim within the running vehicle, instantaneously causing him to divert his glance.

Big Richard had seen a lot of gut-wrenching things throughout the years, but never anything as hideous as what he was currently witnessing. He cringed as the dead man's eyes appeared to be peering clean through Big Richard's soul and directly into his eyes as if to say, "Where were you when I needed your help, old man! And how could you allow this to happen to me in front of your place of business!" He could only assume what his last thoughts could have been.

Big Richard frantically yelled for someone to call 9-1-1 to help appease his guilty conscience, while hurriedly running back inside the store to retrieve his phone. He knew within his heart and mind that the young man was already gone, but still, he never truly wanted to come to grips with the reality of it all. Even though he had observed death many times before, by sight and smell.

He repeatedly dialed everything except 9-1-1 merely out of sheer nervousness until finally getting it right about the seventh try, while shaking as he cradled the phone.

"9-1-1. What's your emergency?" The dispatcher calmly stated in a highly professional tone. She repeated herself when she received no answer. "Hello... Are you there? 9-1-1. What's your emergency?" She calmly recited.

Big Richard finally found his voice. "Send an ambulance to Richard's Market on 40th Avenue North! There's been... there's been a murder! He solemnly explained before unconsciously dropping the receiver in pure disbelief. He looked back at the body in the car and stared into the young man's lifeless eyes. He was unable to look away from the corpse, as a certain incident from his past suddenly began to haunt him once again.

Chapter 27

The bullets missed Taylor's head by mere centimeters, spraying small shards of concrete across her beautiful face. Dozens of tiny nicks and cuts covered her body, from her breast to her head.

Her back ached from awkwardly hitting the pavement when Preston violently tackled her to the ground to get Taylor out of the line of fire. Steel fragments recklessly made contact with almost everything that surrounded them, wounding several innocent bystanders who were in the area at the time, with Preston being amongst the injured.

Huge globs of blood poured from the open wound in Preston's leg like a faucet, making the entire situation appear to be a hundred times worse than what it actually was.

The chaos around them multiplied as women screamed, children cried, and men seethed with anger, demanding answers of any kind and from anybody who had any type of information on the individual who had fired the shots. They were unaware in that moment that the culprit who was responsible for the shooting was already dead.

But that was an entirely different situation all in itself. A problem that neither the police nor the major neighborhood influencers would ever be able to solve. So it was what it was, as most would say, because to some, there was no justice better than street justice, and no one properly understood this analysis better than an individual who had grown up in the urban hoods of Black America.

Preston verbally cursed, swung, kicked, and complained while trying to avoid being taken to the hospital to get some help. "I'm okay! I'm okay!" He continuously chanted towards the EMTs and first responders.

He became agitated with them as they snatched, pulled, sliced, and tugged at his clothing. They cut more fabric from his garments to properly assess the wound, while ignoring all of Preston's demands. They finally got him onto the gurney and into the ambulance.

All of a sudden, Preston had become mysteriously faint and lightheaded. The ambulance workers fought tooth and nail to control the loss of blood.

"Hold on, young man, just hold on, we're almost there, okay!" The EMT worker pleaded with Preston, repeatedly tapping on his cheeks with the back of his hand to keep him coherent and fully awake. Their actions didn't appear to be working out too well for him as Preston's eyelids began to drift almost completely closed, and his breathing became distinguishably sparse and sporadic.

Chapter 28

Taylor jumped into one of the first running vehicles headed in the direction of the hospital, and they closely trailed the ambulance's every move. The ambulance swiftly maneuvered through the city streets of Nashville at a very quick pace. Never once making a complete stop at either traffic lights or stop signs until finally reaching their destination.

Once out of the car and into the hospital, Taylor fought to go to the back with Preston as they hurriedly carted him through the emergency room doors, only to be stopped by two big, burly-looking security guards with a no-nonsense type of demeanor and the physical bearing of an actual serial killer. They abruptly brought her to a screeching halt with the hugeness of just one hand.

Taylor bucked at the men a little in the beginning, raising her voice and becoming somewhat irate, which was obviously pointless. Her small stature was no match for the height and bulkiness of her present opposition. With that being duly noted, Taylor then removed herself from the area altogether, where she began pacing the floor until at least two of her toenails suddenly began to bleed.

Not so much from actually pacing the floor, of course, but more so from banging them against the concrete moments prior, after she and Preston had harshly hit the pavement when the bullets began to fly.

Taylor graciously thanked God once again for Preston's quick-witted survival instincts. She was thankful for how he had chosen her over himself to protect in that moment, which had most definitely saved her life.

Suddenly, she relived everything that she could remember about the entire incident in her head, violently cringing.

Gratitude was an understatement for Taylor in this moment of reflection. But it was also short-lived, due to all of the many soiled and disrespectful looks she was presently receiving from a few women who were there on Preston's behalf as well.

Taylor respectfully tried showing them little to no attention in order to avoid any confrontation. But the obvious daggers the women were hurling in Taylor's direction with their eyes made it almost impossible for her not to respond.

Taylor was an outsider amongst this group of people, and the women didn't mind openly expressing that to her at all. Plus, the fact that she was extremely pretty and very well-endowed for someone so young appeared to have increased these women's jealousy even more.

An allegiance was formed amongst certain individuals who had been blatant enemies for years. But now, they were united, all in the name of their newly inducted foe, which Taylor presumed was her.

Taylor defensively placed her back up against the hospital's waiting room wall, just in case any of them decided to launch an attack. It was apparent that she was outnumbered, and she quickly began surveying the room in search of a familiar face. Someone who would possibly help her out in a tight jam or have her back if fighting ensued.

Then, that's when it suddenly dawned on her. *Where was Mystique?* Taylor quizzically questioned.

She had not physically seen him one single time that day, which was extremely difficult for her to fathom. Especially given how close he and Preston were to one another.

She removed herself from the wall and darted past all of the venomous glares that still watched her like a hawk as she raced outside towards the front of the hospital to check out the vicinity. To her, something was amiss about the entire situation. And a woman's intuition was rarely ever wrong. Especially when those notions were not being dictated by their very own emotions.

Chapter 29

The bleeding finally stopped, and the doctors had thoroughly cleansed the wound, but the pain that Preston felt in that moment was still immensely intolerable. Each and every facial expression that was being displayed on Preston's face described the intensity of the throbbing sensation within the center of his calf muscle. Especially when those movements were unintentional.

Preston winced, but being the type of person who never believed in displaying any weaknesses of any kind, he merely grunted to help conceal his discomfort. He briefly closed his eyes for a short, temporary moment while taking in a few much-needed deep breaths to help mask the pain.

This technique still wasn't working too well. His anger and frustration caused him to grunt a little bit deeper, in hopes of alleviating the irritating agony altogether.

Professionally draped with fresh gauze and bandages, the doctors notified Preston that there was nothing more they could do for the open wound, besides allow it to heal on its own. Which, in due time, it would surely do, they affirmed.

They suggested Preston soak himself in the tub several times a day, with no added substances or soaps to help properly speed up the healing process.

Because at that point, the rest was actually up to God, the doctor stated. He politely shook Preston's hand before handing him his prescribed pain medication and politely pointed him towards a wheelchair, which would be his transportation through the hospital and back to his loved ones. Or at least to whatever chariot that patiently awaited him in the patient pick-up area, the doctor presumed.

But in either case, Preston was now discharged. And the doctor's duties were complete. As Dr. Robertson immersed herself in the massive sea of Black faces, she hurriedly voiced her goodbyes over her shoulder as she went, while rushing back towards the E.R. to help yet another gunshot victim. "What a day. What a day!" Dr. Robertson exclaimed exasperatedly.

The individual on the PA system specifically summoned her by name several times over, bringing Dr. Robertson to an open trot. "I'm coming... I'm coming, dang!" Dr. Robertson repeatedly stated.

She picked up her pace while almost tripping over her very own feet. She surprisingly took a double-take at the young man on the gurney whose throat had been sliced from corner to corner by something extremely sharp. *But how was he still alive?* she wondered.

Dr. Robertson hesitantly trudged forward while saying a silent prayer for the man. Several of her colleagues skillfully worked on Jezebel's young lover until he was partially coherent.

His eyes were wearily searching his surroundings with a look so evil that it instantly made the hairs on the nape of Dr. Robertson's neck and arms stand at full attention. It was as if she were looking at Satan himself firsthand, never fully comprehending the fact that in that moment and time, she actually was!

Chapter 30

The doctors consistently worked on Jezebel's young lover as if his life depended on it. Because in that moment, it did. Perspiration dampened the doctor's scrubs as sweat poured from their pores, creating huge circles on their sleeves from wiping every droplet with their forearms. They worked themselves into a frenzy while trying to save the young man's life.

Voices were raised, commands were hurled, and utensils were meticulously handled as stitch after stitch was being applied to the young lover's throat. He would be left with a scar so hideous across his windpipe, which resembled the sinisterness of the Joker's smile.

But he was still alive, and that's all that truly mattered, each doctor solemnly agreed. Shortly after the doctors were done, they gave one another several celebratory high-fives on a job well done. There was honestly no better feeling in the world for a doctor than actually saving someone's life.

Especially after bringing him back from the dead, which was exactly what the young lovers' previous fate was, as the eerie-sounding monitor displayed that he'd flatlined three times until finally recapturing a pulse.

The doctors stabilized the patient and thoroughly scrubbed themselves down before exiting the operating room. The head surgeon then notified his staff to prepare a secluded area for the victim. A place with little to almost no outside access, just in case his life was still in danger.

The last thing any of them needed to be dealing with at the time was some sadistic nutcase trying to finish a job they had failed to carry out only hours prior. That was something they could neither afford nor stomach, for that matter, both doctors and nurses fully agreed.

The charge nurse quickly followed the doctor's orders, locating the most deserted wing of the hospital before discreetly entering Jezebel's young lover into the computer's database as a John Doe to further conceal his identity.

The mere thought of taking all these precautions in this situation had Nurse Coffee jittery and far more nervous than usual.

With shaky hands, she summoned the very best and most reliable members of the hospital's security team to help safely carry out this mission. Just anybody wouldn't do, Nurse Coffee confidently believed. She wasn't taking any chances.

Entering the operating room herself, for the very first time since the surgery, she walked hesitantly with both security guards extremely close in proximity, as she escorted the young lover's body to his awaiting room. She couldn't tear her eyes away from the scar as she sadly asked herself, or better yet, asked him the question, "My God, young man, what did you do?"

To her surprise, what happened next nearly caused Nurse Coffee to have a heart attack. She fell back into one of the security guard's huge arms, desperately gasping for air.

Dread filled her as she locked eyes with Jezebel's young lover, who now stared back at her, his piercing gaze wickedly searing straight through her soul with what appeared to be one evil glance before he subconsciously drifted back to wherever it was that he had just recently emerged from, spiritually.

Neither security guard witnessed a thing.

Chapter 31

Time heals all wounds, most would say. But in this case, it would not.

Not for Preston.

Not for Taylor.

And not for Jezebel's young lover either.

He had miraculously made it out of the hospital and was somewhere, lying low while diligently plotting, planning, prepping, and orchestrating his very next move.

It definitely wasn't over. Not by a long shot, he silently professed.

He repeatedly rubbed his scar, seething each time his fingers brushed against it, while struggling to adapt to his new, barely audible voice. Every attempt to speak fueled his rage even more.

Everything was a complete blur for the young lover at first, and he couldn't understand why. But as the hours morphed into days, and days somehow into weeks, his memory gradually began to return.

But what he couldn't figure out for the life of him at the moment was, "Where the heck was Jezebel? And why hadn't she ever come to see him when he was in the hospital?" he muttered aloud, his voice raspy and broken.

He was unaware that hospital policy had forbidden visitors of any kind due to the seriousness of the crime. That small detail messed with his mind, feeding his paranoia and frustration even more.

A billion scenarios bombarded his thoughts at the time. But nothing more prominent than, "Was she alright?"

Worryingly, he massaged his head and face in frustration, repetitively asking the question over and over again as though the empty room could give him an answer that never came.

"Well, is she? Is she, Lord? Is she!" The newly nervous young lover cried out.

He had no earthly idea that Jezebel herself had been the one who was blatantly responsible for setting him up. She was the mastermind behind the foiled attempt that had almost permanently cost him his life.

At that very moment, Jezebel moaned at the top of her lungs in pure satisfaction while Mystique pummeled into her from behind.

Mystique showed the much older specimen no mercy as he violently plunged into her.

Jezebel cried out from the pain, biting into the first thing her mouth could reach, as Mystique pushed her head deeper into the mattress, assaulting her womb even more as she pleasurably whined.

She gradually submitted to his strength as he physically held her in place with one hand, while aggressively pulling her hair. Jezebel begged him to explode through muffled cries, and Mystique obliged without hesitation.

Grunting, growling, and partially howling himself, he released his jism all over Jezebel's back and buttocks, trying to skeet it into her hair as he devilishly grinned.

Chapter 32

Mystique figured things would feel a little off when he finally emerged from the shadows again. But he never imagined it to be as awkward as it was. Complete silence encompassed the entire room once he crossed the threshold of his best friend's mother's door.

The energy had shifted instantly, and he could tell by the looks on their faces as he made his way toward his friend. He was briefly stopped along the way by Preston's mother, whose hug felt more like a slight search, rather than her normally warm embrace. The realization caused Mystique to cringe inside due to her recent lack of trust.

But how could he blame her? Especially when her son had previously been attacked by some unknown foe, he reasoned in silence.

He quickly channeled his undivided attention back on the main task at hand, restructuring his game face for all to see.

Confidently, he stood taller than ever before, head held high, as he came into contact with his partner, never truly knowing what to say or do in the moment as he leaned in for a hug.

The embrace between the two men was similar to that with Preston's mother, though not quite as cold. Preston performed the exact same pat-down technique, just in a different way. It shattered Mystique internally, vividly confirming the blatant distrust his best friend now had for him. He acknowledged that he was to blame, yet it still hurt; he had to admit, even if he didn't truly show it at the time.

He suddenly began battling with himself to find the right words, hoping to somehow break the tension, while looking his partner directly in the eyes as he began to speak.

Preston was extremely smart, and Mystique fully understood that he had to be careful. Not only with his approach, but also with his choice of words.

He knew that he was standing before the one person who could read him like a book, even when no one else was able to. So he made sure to keep things brief.

He only spoke when spoken to. The only thing was, at the moment, Preston didn't really have too much to say. So he preferred to listen.

This caused another awkward moment between the two best friends, which Mystique had to expeditiously lay to rest, especially if he didn't want to lose the trust of his partner in crime. In that moment, by the look in Preston's eyes, things weren't looking too promising for Mystique.

Mystique had seen that look many times before, but he had never been on the receiving end of his disappointment. He was more than happy when Taylor finally approached with a smile. She asked both men if they'd like anything to eat or drink, and they both respectfully declined.

Taylor read Preston's energy and intervened, asking Mystique for some assistance carrying some chairs, vowing to Preston that she wasn't trying to steal his best friend. She smiled and walked away, with Mystique cleverly taking that as his cue to leave. He headed straight for the exit as soon as he and Taylor rounded the corner, where no one else could see or hear them speak.

But not before escaping Taylor's question. "Where have you been, Mystique?" Taylor asked forwardly with no hesitation. She skeptically observed Preston's best friend as he slightly avoided the question altogether and switched the topic.

"Look, I can't disclose the details of what I'm currently doing right now, but eventually y'all will understand. So, when that time comes, just be prepared to do whatever it is that you gotta do." Mystique forewarned Taylor. "Because I definitely will be, and that's a promise!" He added.

He left Taylor completely dumbfounded by the boldness of his words as he confidently strolled away, jumping into a tinted vehicle with a woman whose silhouette strongly resembled that of her very own mother.

The woman distinctly tapped the horn at Taylor several times over while throwing up the deuce sign, as they gradually drove away.

Chapter 33

Jezebel watched as Taylor tried to look inside the vehicle as she slowly eased forward to conceal her identity. She didn't want to truly let the rabbit out of the hat yet. The surprise that she had in store for her daughter and Preston was definitely going to be a doozie, she evilly grinned.

And with Mystique on her side, Jezebel knew there was no way on earth that she could fail.

She cranked the volume up on her Bose' surround sound system just a few more notches as she hit the gas, pushing the speedometer well over 80 mph. The legal street mileage was only 45 mph, and she never intended to stop for anyone until finally reaching her destination. Even if the law were to jump behind her.

Mystique was never much of a talker to begin with, but at the moment, he was exceptionally quiet. There was one thing that he couldn't seem to get out of his mind, which was the disappointment in his partner's eyes.

Noticing the spaced-out look on Mystique's face, Jezebel intervened. Although treading lightly, she gingerly began to spit her spill, while pretending that she was actually interested in what was troubling him at that moment, when she truly was not.

But hey, at least she was pretending to care, she admitted. She was smiling to herself due to her previous thoughts, while skillfully massaging Mystique's inner thigh, hoping that the constant blood flow, which was now filling up his partially hardened member, would somehow change his mind. But honestly, it did not.

Mystique realized exactly what Jezebel was up to and grabbed her hand, squeezing it tightly, until suddenly he released his grip, apologizing to her for his aggressiveness as she softly winced.

"Sorry, Ms. Lady, just got a lot on my mind right now, that's all. You forgive me, right?" Mystique smoothly asked, kissing the spot upon her hand that he'd hurt with much tenderness. Jezebel began to relent, releasing juices from places that made her feel very much alive in that moment. She hurriedly found a secluded place to park. She straddled the dangerous young lion that occupied the passenger side of her car.

She bucked, gyrated, and grinded her way to ecstasy under the cold and watchful stares of her extremely pissed-off ex-lover. His anger appeared to have increased every time he touched the hideousness of his lengthy scar!

He solemnly vowed to leave a permanently new fissure of skin tissue somewhere upon her body, while quickly brandishing his new weapon.

He checked all cylinders to make sure that each of the chambers was fully loaded, and he desperately tried to make his way to Jezebel's vehicle undetected.

But to no avail. A much older Caucasian couple blew his cover after visibly noticing the pistol.

"Hey buddy! What on earth are you doing, young man? Get outta here before I call the cops!" The older gentleman loudly yelped.

The older guy reached for his phone as the ex-lover urgently evaded the scene, cursing the entire way, as he desperately ran.

Chapter 34

Huffing and puffing while desperately trying to get away, the young ex-lover could still vividly hear the older man's screams echoing in his head. He was paranoid and highly pissed off as he rapidly fled.

Today was obviously not the day for Jezebel to finally meet with her Maker, he thought. But best believe it was coming soon. The young ex-lover promised himself this as he gathered his fishing equipment, cautiously surveyed the scene.

And to think, he hadn't even been searching for Jezebel yet. Oh, but look how God always seemed to make a way, he thought with a sinister grin.

He flanked the remainder of his fishing poles over his left shoulder, while carrying a bucket full of fish with his right hand, he continuously checked his six often than not as he skeptically moved along.

Finally making it back to his place of seclusion, the young ex-lover hurriedly packed his belongings, desperately trying to make it back to the city to finish what he started.

And finish it he would, he solemnly promised himself in all sincerity. Even if it meant losing his very own life in the process.

Vivid scenes of Jezebel's whorish acts scorched through the young man's brain, permanently etching images into his memory, whether he wanted them there or not.

He dangerously swerved in and out of traffic at a breakneck speed, yet still handled the vehicle extremely well. The young ex-lover's memory re-emerged in full bloom, causing him to slam on the brakes, smack dead in the middle of the interstate with vehicles moving all around him.

Cars swerved. Semi-trucks fishtailed. Horns blared. All while trying to stop. Curse words were hurled. Middle fingers were displayed with the deadliest of intentions. But the young man never witnessed a thing. His mind was elsewhere, replaying everything that had happened several weeks prior.

Then bam!

That's when it hit him!

Especially the part pertaining to the keys. And how they'd openly been left lying on the floor behind locked doors. His entire body flushed red with anger, although his original skin tone was an almond brown. Fumes rose from his body like smoke from a smoldering fire as Jezebel's young ex-lover finally connected all of the dots, which totally devastated him after realizing that it was she who had not only set him up but had also tried to get him killed.

Just as she'd tried to do to Preston and Taylor, the young ex-lover acknowledged.

"Dirty Wench!"

Chapter 35

Chaos engulfed everyone, and no one was exempt from Jezebel's fury. Not even herself. Her extremely vindictive ways were beginning to come home to roost, as Malcolm X once stated to the press, while being asked about the JFK assassination that occurred in Dallas, Texas, which not only changed his life and current circumstances forever, but also led to a drastic change in his mindset in a very drastic way. Especially after his pilgrimage to Mecca, it was stated.

Jezebel felt something looming within her spirit that she just couldn't quite detect, but she knew it was weighing her down. She felt as if someone was watching her, never realizing that someone definitely was. Her young ex-lover steadily studied her every step of the way, meticulously plotting the perfect strike, not only on Jezebel, but on Mystique as well. The very person that the young ex-lover's instincts were telling him was solely responsible for trying to kill him by savagely slicing his throat.

He was more than positive that Mystique's actions were all a part of Jezebel's devilish scheme. After all, just look at what she'd manipulated him into doing to Preston and her very own daughter, he thought. His mind reverted to the day that everything had taken place, and how adamant Jezebel had become about him seeking revenge, figuring that she could kill several birds with one stone, without her ever lifting a finger. After intentionally filling his young heart and head with malice, she urgently pushed open his door.

But she never intended for him to survive. But somehow, he actually did.

He took everything in, finally realizing the ugly truth about the woman he loved, who proclaimed to have loved him back. The young ex-lover's blood pressure levels spiked from anger. Especially after realizing that he had walked right past Mystique, with a pistol in hand, just before the shooting had occurred.

He now knew for a fact that it was him, because he could never forget those eyes, which were the very same deadly set of eyes that were coldly staring back at him from the back seat of his vehicle through the rearview mirror. Just before everything went black.

Chapter 36

Adversity surrounded Preston from every angle, but he never allowed it to interfere with his mental state. Even after hearing all of the rumors that involved Jezebel and Mystique. He refused to believe the rumors until he received some pictures from an unknown source of the two eating together, laughing, holding hands, and even worse, being intimate. Preston continuously flipped through flick after flick, and seeing those images turned Taylor's stomach. Preston carefully observed Taylor's every move to see if she was involved.

After all, she was Jezebel's daughter, he thought.

With Mystique switching up on him because of a woman, Preston truly didn't know who to trust. So, from that point on, he wasn't taking any chances. Especially seeing that the one person whom he had genuinely called brother for so many years was now possibly betraying him, as well.

Taylor could sense Preston's angst and gently caressed his hand. She was talking to his inner turmoil without ever speaking a word, like only she could do.

Her touch instantly quieted the noise inside him and settled his spirit, causing him to smile. He wondered what it was about the woman who occupied his space.

Preston bounced his feet as positive energy suddenly surged through his body. Smiling at Taylor with only his eyes, she pleasantly reciprocated his thoughts, understanding in that moment that words were no longer necessary.

Taylor knew exactly what Preston needed, and she physically provided it through a simple touch. This assured him that he wasn't alone. He telepathically received her message with full understanding. Preston confidently headed for the door, ready for whatever, by any means necessary, even if it consisted of war.

He double-checked his attire to ensure that everything was copacetic. Preston shifted and unshifted certain objects because taking another bullet was no longer a part of his regimen.

And he meant that with all of his heart.

Preston began strolling through his neighborhood fully healed, feeling stronger than ever. He kindly greeted his elders and gave the kids in the neighborhood dollars for snacks as if nothing had ever changed.

Because truthfully, it hadn't.

Not even the fact that he was still being watched by several different sets of eyes, for many different reasons. But none of them could have ever known Preston better than his so-called brother from the same struggle, Mystique.

The one and only person who could truly sink his ship or knock him off his throne entirely, Jezebel believed.

Chapter 37

Preston knew that the streets were waiting to see how he would respond after being attacked. Or how he would handle his best friend's behavior, for that matter. But as always, he played it smooth, remaining cooler than the other side of the pillow, something older southern folks loved to say.

Preston knew that this situation was definitely chess, not checkers. This was something he'd always been told about situations such as these. So it was imperative for him to constantly stay three steps ahead, and five to ten steps ahead of his enemies.

Doing the right thing wasn't always easy for Preston, but he believed it was more than necessary.

And he wasn't just speaking in terms of how the world currently viewed what was right or wrong because over time, he'd come to realize that so many different types of things pertained to what was considered right. Especially when you were Black in America, he emphasized.

Preston viewed his surroundings with a mass amount of joy and sadness all combined. Joy from all of the love and camaraderie that presently engulfed him while surveying the everyday comings and goings of his community. And sadness because of how the government intentionally forced most of his people to live. Which wasn't much of a living for them at all, to be honest.

But somehow, his people managed to make the best of it because that's just what Black people did.

Preston smiled at his latter thoughts, but his smile suddenly faded into a scowl, knowing that he could possibly become a blatant hypocrite to some of his very own beliefs. Beliefs that would potentially cause him to have to hurt his so-called brother, his best friend, or any other person of African descent, if they pushed him to that point. Preston fully understood this firsthand, but if he was forced, he would with no hesitation.

A shivering chill went down Preston's spine as certain images flashed within his mind. Images and scenes that completely bawled his insides into tight little knots. He violently shook his head in hopes of erasing the thoughts altogether. Thoughts that physically made him sick to his stomach, causing his mouth to rapidly fill with saliva.

Spitting several times over, Preston refused to swallow the fluids, knowing that it would make him puke. And the last thing that he needed at that moment was someone inquiring about whether or not he was okay. Huge droplets of sweat began pouring from his scalp and down his face as if he'd run a couple of miles at full speed, which was the furthest thing from the truth at that time, because physically, Preston hadn't moved an inch.

He couldn't move. Not at the moment, at least, because his thoughts wouldn't allow it. This was something that doctors called psychomotor retardation. A condition where your mental and physical activities are completely slowed down, often manifesting as sluggish body movements due to a slowing of thought processes. This was exactly what the images of him physically harming Mystique, or vice versa, had caused him to do from every physical aspect. Preston couldn't hold it any longer. Vomit began oozing from his mouth like that of an open faucet, accompanied by the awful stench, stankily plastering onto the pavement, splashing small particles of unrecognizable fragments upon his sneakers.

"Why, homie? Why!" Preston asked in disbelief, shaking his head for the thousandth time.

He was truly hurting inside, unable to fully comprehend what was going on between him and his partner, or what had actually gone wrong. Anger instantly began replacing his grief.

Fervidly understanding that he might have to discontinue the life of his best friend. He knew that Mystique wouldn't really give him much of a choice if it actually came to that. Especially with his kill or be killed mentality, Preston thought, inadvertently shaking his head at how stupid all of this was. Preston's mind visibly diverted back towards the individual who was technically responsible, Jezebel.

As a vivid image of Jezebel's devilish face, deceitfully grinning in the most conniving of ways, quickly re-entered Preston's memory.

"Deceptive Wench!" he said.

Chapter 38

Preston was mentally conflicted, while internally being pulled in every possible direction. Sensing that Taylor could somehow automatically detect his inner angst, he did everything within his power to conceal his deepest, most troublesome thoughts. Her abilities were more than partially true in a sense. Taylor stared him directly in the eyes, reading him like a fortune-teller as he guiltily looked away. Preston knew that what was coursing through his mind at the time was definitely not good for either of them!

There was an ugliness brewing within Preston's spirit that was almost impossible to control. One that he felt just had to be released. He physically met Taylor's eyes head-on without blinking, cautiously warning her as he continuously stared.

Taylor felt the animosity and chose to keep her distance. She knew that she could reach him better with her words, so she softly spoke, clearly utilizing a scripture that she once learned from the Bible. It stated that, "A soft answer turns away wrath, but a harsh word stirs up anger."

And with all of the testosterone that was flowing through Preston's body at that moment, she knew the latter part of Proverbs 15:1 was truly not an option for her.

Taylor eased herself closer and closer to this raging young bull before gently placing a hand upon his chest. Instantaneously eradicating certain thoughts of her and only her within his mind, while his cruel and vengeful thoughts towards Jezebel and Mystique continuously loomed. Especially after revisiting the images from the pictures.

Preston started to speak but stopped, silencing himself instead. He was taught that a wisdom-filled man was never to speak out of anger or emotions.

He physically closed his eyes in brief meditation, while quietly reiterating the impact of his grandfather's words. Words that just so happened to place him right back on his square.

Preston apologized to Taylor for his aggression. But what he felt for Jezebel and Mystique was etched in stone. Just like the words that were written on the tablets that Moses presented to the children of Israel on Mount Sinai.

And that was Law!

"Because thou shall never cross your partner, or side with a blatant enemy over Preston!" He stated seriously. He reached for the object that was secretly concealed in his waistband when someone loudly tapped on the living room door. The sound unexpectedly caught them both by surprise, and Taylor's eyes instinctively followed his hands.

"Certified Package Delivery!" The UPS carrier yelled, notifying him that he needed a signature, in the midst of Preston quickly snatching open the door. The UPS carrier was puzzled by his promptness. Preston quickly scribbled his name upon realizing, just as before, that the package was once again addressed to him, but it still had no return address.

"What the...?" Preston confusingly ranted, knowing that it was probably something that he didn't wanna see. Nor hear for that matter, as he skeptically tore open the package.

Chapter 39

Slowly easing open the cardboard container, Preston noticed that it was some type of recording device or camera thingy of some kind. He peeled back the wrappings and took every precaution possible to make sure that no part of the package's inner contents came in contact with his skin. He meticulously handled the modernized camcorder until he was positive it was safe.

Not only for himself, but for Taylor as well.

There had been many instances where substances such as anthrax and many other unknown deadly pathogens were being used to silently take out enemies by simply touching or inhaling the particles. Preston knew that he wasn't taking any chances.

He carefully removed the device from its box, keeping it at arm's length with the least amount of movement. He hurriedly covered his mouth, nose, and hands with the first credible piece of fabric that physically caught his eye, purposely taking the shortest of shortest breaths as he continued onward.

When he realized that everything was copacetic, Preston gestured for Taylor to come closer so that they could check out what had been sent. He was praying to God that whatever it was, it wasn't any more bad news. He hesitantly pressed play.

But oh, what a surprise they both received when the footage began to roll, especially when the cameraman professionally zoomed in on Mystique's focused face, as he secretly observed Preston's every move. He watched as Mystique performed the very same tactics with the gun that was tightly clutched within his best friend's hand, skillfully checking his weapon.

Mystique was making sure that the gun was properly cleaned and ready for when it was time for him to use it. Preston angrily watched, realizing exactly what he was doing firsthand at that moment. Those were normally things that they'd both done together at least a thousand times. According to what Preston was witnessing, it would obviously be their very last now.

Acting on instinct, Preston dropped his hand back to his waistline once again, but this time, he did not care what Taylor thought or had to say. In that moment, his mind became overly saturated with WAR!

And it wouldn't be appeased until it was actually compensated with blood, Preston thought. He physically felt all of his animalistic instincts overpower him as his aggressive nature caused him to gurgle inside. He released a loud growling sound from somewhere deep within as if he was possessed.

Taylor stared in fear without moving a muscle until finally getting close enough to him to tenderly grab his hands. Her physical touch temporarily calmed the inner beast inside, in a sense. But not long enough.

Preston openly admitted that he was no longer his brother's keeper.

Certain stories from the Bible began vividly displaying within his mind for some strange reason, especially Genesis 4:1-16, the story of Cain and Abel.

It was a perfect depiction of what was actually happening in Preston's life at the time. Definitely the part pertaining to a jealous brother!

But unlike Abel, Preston thought, the voice of his blood would not crieth out unto the Lord from the ground, especially if it was up to him!

Chapter 40

The young ex-lover's plan was unfolding perfectly, as he physically sowed discord among all parties involved, turning them against one another more and more, while continuously filling each of their hearts and minds with false illusions and expectations that appeared to be real. His plan was defined as nothing more than lies. The young ex-lover genuinely smiled, truthfully loving every moment of the chaos that he was creating, which he planned to do until the very end. Or at least until Preston and Mystique were both physically dead and finally resting in their graves. He proudly relished at the idea.

He didn't really care too much about Taylor at all during that time. Truthfully, she served him no purpose, at least not at that moment. But who knows, maybe someday she eventually would, he thought, especially if things didn't work out the way that he was expecting between Preston and Mystique. They had definitely been more than his top priority after finding out that they were responsible for the fatal slaying of his big cousin Ron, thanks to Jezebel.

She was the one and only woman that he'd ever truly loved in his life, besides his mother. And the only other woman who had ever truly loved him back. Even if she wasn't fully aware that she did at the time. Jezebel's love for him was something he delusionally rationalized in his mind.

He was physically tracing the outline of Jezebel's body with his index finger, tenderly caressing her picture. He tightly closed his eyes while mimicking her moans, as if she were actually present. He became extremely pissed off after coming in contact with his very own hand and realizing she was not really there. He aggressively blamed Mystique for taking his Jezebel away.

He thought she surely would never just up and leave him on her own. The young ex-lover truly made himself believe.

Leaving the front door to his disclosed location completely ajar, he rapidly rushed to the stolen vehicle, preparing for war just in case it actually came down to that. But he knew that he definitely wasn't living another single day without his woman, regardless of what anyone else may have believed in that present moment.

He aimlessly careened the stolen vehicle with no tags to Jezebel's last known place of residence. He was hoping and praying for some resistance of any kind while passionately clutching his pistol.

There was no stronger fury than a mentally deranged, broken-hearted, young ex-lover, which clearly exceeded any comparisons to that of a woman scorned. Simply due to the unrestricted acts of violent thoughts that merely existed in a young man's heart, especially when he's been manipulated and deceived.

Better yet, what about almost being technically killed! He thought.

Chapter 41

A storm was presently brewing, in which everyone was now involved. Even several innocent bystanders, as there had been before. And the sad thing about it all was, only God would be able to predict each of their undetermined fates. The foiled egos of all the men connected to this terrible debacle were only seeing red!

Even Preston, who had more than mentally lost his peaceful way and positivity, solely due to the devious actions of his present foes. Especially when it came to those he knew by name, Jezebel and Mystique.

They were the two individuals that he sacredly vowed to extract vengeance upon if it was the last thing he did on God's green earth. That was a promise that Preston intended to keep.

He deeply cringed at the mere thought of their names, causing his mind to travel further and further into the abyss. A place where common sense or rational thinking no longer mattered or existed, especially when interacting with demons, Preston concurred.

He fully submerged himself into the depths of his inner darkness with no resistance, hoping that it was enough to emerge from it all victoriously without it totally tarnishing his soul. But if not, then at least he'd have company. Preston figured there was no way on earth that he wasn't dragging them both right into hell with him on this first-class flight. Even if it costs him his life.

Preston massaged the deepened wrinkles of his scrunched-up brow as he angrily scowled.

Known for always mentally keeping it together in a sense, Preston had now traded in his normally demure type of personality for one of pure barbarism. But still, he constantly calculated his every move like that of a world-renowned master of chess. Subsequently, he established the perfect plan in order to personally annihilate his enemies, figuratively meaning that in every sense of the word.

He carefully sheathed the exceptionally sharpened blade in its holster while meticulously doing the same with his twin MC9 LS Canik handguns. Then he laced his waistline with a few extra clips, just in case things became a little more tragic than usual.

All of this strangely felt good to Preston for some inexplicable reason as he began to justify his previous actions behind it all. He was doing whatever possible on his behalf to try and make everything make sense while comparing himself to several high-ranking officials within the military.

After all, there had been several generals, captains, and sergeants of war who had also used certain tactics of manipulation to purposely fill their soldiers' minds with whatever was necessary for certain missions to be carried out or successfully accomplished. This tactic had been shaped and based on lies for the so-called common good of all the American people. In which we also know that it never involved, nor was it ever intended to benefit the overall plight of Black people.

Pre or Post Slavery!

These things were still happening to Blacks even hundreds of years later. But that is a completely different story all in itself, Preston gloomily thought.

Due to the shifting of his already troublesome thoughts, this suddenly created a newly found surge of energy within his mind, while linking them to that of Jezebel and Mystique. Within Preston's mind, they had become even more traitorous to their people than William O'Neal.

William O'Neal was the FBI informant who infiltrated the Black Panther Party and set up Fred Hampton for assassination in 1969.

Boiling internally, Preston no longer needed to try and justify anything. He had no plans to show any mercy when extracting his revenge.

He panoramically pictured his enemies falling over and over again within his mind, as he violently hunted them both down like deer on an open terrain, never actually squeezing the trigger until finally getting the perfect shot.

Preston gloated over the images of his imagination and proudly smiled, just before suddenly becoming extremely saddened in his heart and mind.

His sadness didn't come from what he'd thought about within his mind. That was something he actually didn't care about at all. But he did actually care about the sadness in Taylor's eyes.

Images of her sudden gloom vividly popped up within Preston's mind, which totally made him feel completely terrible in a sense.

But what Taylor never found out, Preston would never admit to or ever discuss with anyone other than God. Point. Blank. Period!

Chapter 42

A loud and extremely obnoxious knock on the door quickly brought Mystique to his feet with a weapon in hand, as Jezebel desperately scrambled to cover her naked frame. She instinctively scanned the room for anything else out of the ordinary that she needed to conceal at the moment. She thought it definitely had to be the cops, especially with a knock like that.

She trembled a little inside as she fought to gather her thoughts. Knowing that she would have to be on top of her game. As she has said before, jail was definitely not an option for her. Nor was it a part of her future plans. And Jezebel truthfully meant that with all of her heart.

She became more and more paranoid with every fleeting moment, as Mystique stood as still as a board beside the living room door. He remained as quiet as possible while anxiously waiting to hear something from the other side of the door. But nothing ever came.

Mystique's heart continuously pounded within his chest as he began hand-signaling Jezebel, notifying her that the coast was clear. Or so he thought. He hesitantly eased his eye towards the peephole to sneak a peek, hoping that a surprise in the shape of a bullet wasn't awaiting him on the other end as he skeptically did so. With all of the scandalous and low-down things that they'd repeatedly done together over the past few months, one never could truly tell.

He released a small sigh of relief after making his attempt, as small sweat beads had rapidly begun congregating in such places that were known for producing a putrid stench. Especially if not handled in a timely manner.

Mystique secretly performed a quick wellness check on himself, making sure that he was physically good before easing the door open to retrieve the unidentified package with no return address.

The package appeared to be almost identical in looks, shape, and size to that which was sent to Preston and Taylor just a short time prior. Jezebel's young ex-lover watched from a distance as Mystique retrieved the package and extensively grinned.

He was absolutely loving all of the possible chaos and commotion that was sure to transpire from the footage that was being deceptively shared on his behalf, and he had no intention of stopping until all involved parties violently ceased to exist.

All except for Jezebel, of course, whom he definitely planned to torture and immensely punish himself. He knew she had to be punished after hearing her openly confess to Mystique about how it turned her on just knowing that he'd slit her ex-lover's throat and evilly allowed him to die.

With Jezebel having no earthly idea about his present resurrection, the young ex-lover sinisterly smiled.

Because in his case, it actually didn't take him a full three days to rise, due to the fact that God had merely blessed him by bringing him back amongst the living that very same day.

But it wasn't to fulfill God's purpose, in which the young ex-lover believed, but then again, maybe it actually was. He sinisterly grinned for a second time, gladly thinking of nothing but death!

Chapter 43

The plot was steadily thickening, and most of their hearts were now almost immensely blackened as Jezebel's young ex-lover continuously added more and more coals to an already overheated furnace.

He laughed like a maniac at the top of his damaged larynx, which still released little to no sounds, as he sneeringly grimaced. Hearing how he sounded, he truly missed the deepness of his old baritone voice even more, which filled his whole body with rage.

"So today was definitely going to be the day that each of their lives drastically took a turn for the worse," he solemnly vowed to himself.

What he planned for them, their lives would be far worse than his life had turned during the past several weeks, he wickedly thought. He observed himself in the floor-length mirror as he stared at his handsome face and the extremely hideous, disturbing-looking flesh that now adorned the front of his neckline. He dementedly posed with the weapon, as he sadistically rubbed it against his scar.

Jezebel's young ex-lover pleasurably smiled from ear to ear at the touch of the cold, hard steel. He instantly reverted his young, feeble mind back to their last love-making session and violently punched the glass, shattering it into a thousand pieces. He appeared to be more and more fascinated with his very own blood, wishing that it was actually Preston's, Jezebel's, or Mystique's. He vaguely attempted to nurse his wounds, mesmerized by the deep, rich red hue, as small particles of his DNA splattered onto the carpet, staining it for dear life.

Just as Preston's, Jezebel's, and Mystique's blood would also stain the pavement that caught their fallen bodies, when the time finally came for their demise. That moment was something Jezebel's young ex-lover was truly looking forward to with open arms. Their demise would happen either by his hands or that of their very own, he thought.

To him, it really didn't matter, as long as it happened and happened quickly.

He was tired of them still residing amongst the living, especially with no major ailments or disturbing disfigurements like he was forced to view every day when he looked into the mirror. He definitely had to change that for them and change it permanently!

While implementing the last and final parts of his well-thought-out scheme, he hoped that he wouldn't physically have to hurt Taylor's GiGi too bad. But if push came to shove, he most definitely would!

Chapter 44

Taylor kept seeing a strange car continuously drive back and forth past her GiGi's home, but she thought nothing of it at first. That is, until she finally got a better look at the individual behind the wheel. His face was one that she would never forget in her life. She suddenly jumped to her feet in order to notify her GiGi of his presence, but she quickly realized that her grandmother was no longer at home.

And that's when Taylor saw *her*, smiling happily as if she had not a single care in the world. Taylor cringed, unaware of whom she was speaking with at the time. The individual who shot at her and Preston weeks prior cruised along and gingerly waved his hand at Taylor, cynically winking his eye, while silently mouthing for her to contact Preston.

She felt an awkward disturbance within her spirit, which instantly placed her in a very precarious type of situation. Jezebel's young ex-lover casually winked his eye at Taylor once again, allowing her to see that he had the upper hand.

Or so he thought.

Taylor's heart instantly fell into her stomach, cramping as if she was about to come on her cycle, knowing that she was possibly about to lose someone extremely dear to her heart.

Taylor muzzled her screams with her shirt to help conceal her frustrations from her grandmother's nosey neighbors. The last thing she needed was for people to start gossiping or formulating all sorts of fabricated stories.

She desperately tried to gather her thoughts while calling on her deceased father for some much-needed wisdom. She knew that, deceased or not, he would surely guide her on how to deal with the situation, and that was something she rightfully believed.

And as always, he never let her down.

An answer quickly bombarded her mind, one that could literally save both GiGi and Preston's lives. Although she would be sacrificing her very own life in the process, she knew she was willing to make that sacrifice.

She quickly headed towards the bottom of the hill to find Preston, whom she knew would be in total disapproval of her plan. But she knew what had to be, just had to be, and she didn't care if he did not approve.

She understood that some things just needed a woman's touch.

Jezebel hadn't taught her much of anything else, but she definitely taught Taylor and her siblings how to be very persuasive and extremely manipulative to a fault.

Somehow, she believed that part of her had been deeply embedded in her bloodline. It was now time for her to utilize some of her mother's extremely vindictive tactics, and she would skillfully use them to her advantage, Taylor thought.

When it came to protecting the people that she loved, she would do whatever was necessary. Realizing that her loved ones now included Preston, she questioned herself about how she could love him when they'd never even physically hugged or kissed.

Yet and still, just knowing that she actually did love him, and surprisingly enough, she was about to figure out exactly why. Because their bond, soul ties, and blatant connection to one another was truly deeper than one could ever mentally imagine.

Chapter 45

Finding Preston had not been an easy task for Taylor, but she eventually located him, preparing himself for war. He quickly discarded the weapons from his hands, passing them to Lil Gary and Bay. Two more of his most trusted cronies, who always argued like cats and dogs, but had one another's back to a fault, in the same way that he and Mystique had been at one point, Preston vividly remembered.

A blatant mixture of anger, hatred, love, and disappointment presented itself upon Preston's handsome face, distorting the image of his once extremely caring eyes. Preston stared past Taylor, unable to look her directly in the eyes as she verbally explained her plan. He only captured certain words escaping her lips as she continued to speak, because for him, none of it made any sense at all. Especially the parts where she was speaking of immersing herself into this arduous combustion of chaos, which more than likely could have an outcome of death.

Not only for Preston, Jezebel, Mystique, or Jezebel's apparently deranged young ex-lover, but also for Taylor. This was something that Preston would never consent to in no shape, form, or fashion. Nor would he ever allow it to happen as long as he still had breath in his body, he thought.

Preston was flattered at Taylor's undying commitment towards him, but also somewhat baffled by it. After all, they barely even knew each other. So that part he didn't fully understand until he realized that he'd instinctively done the exact same thing for her to keep her out of harm's way. His thoughts suddenly caused an unexplainable warmth within his heart that had never existed before, not even in the presence of his mother.

Preston briefly basked in the feeling before coming back to his senses. He was steadily disputing with Taylor about what should or shouldn't be done when it came to being a woman. Taylor interrupted the back and forth with just a simple touch of her hand, realizing how pointless it was to go back and forth with a man who was filled with so much pride and ego.

Taylor smiled as she instinctively utilized a tactic from her mother's very descriptive handbook of lies and manipulation. One that tended to work every single time.

An extremely hazardous ruse that she'd consistently witnessed her mother perform on her father several times during the years. She softly reiterated her plan to Preston in full detail until he conceded to the true genius of her scheme due to the fact that her plan was actually that darn good.

Preston knew that he was being finessed, and although he knew it, her cunningness still reigned supreme. Placing a strong sense of euphoria in the pit of his gut that resonated with what most users had normally described after sniffing their first bump of heroin. Which had to be dangerously addictive in every possible facet known to man if it felt anything even remotely close to what he was currently feeling at the time

Preston enjoyed the euphoria for a little while longer, wishing it never had to end because he knew that what he felt at the moment was far better than what awaited him on every corner, cut, or in every darkened hiding spot of his community.

All the places where his opposition would most likely dwell, especially individuals such as Mystique and Jezebel. So for Preston, he knew that it was imperative that he kept his head on a swivel and his pistol in his hand. Because as much as he instinctively knew about his ex-best friend's patterns, Preston could never truthfully say that he'd learned everything about him. Especially when he hadn't even learned everything about himself yet, to be honest.

So, with that being the conclusion of it all in a nutshell, Preston hurriedly fixated his mind back on war, blocking out every great feeling that Taylor had just placed inside of him, especially if he planned on surviving this very tumultuous ordeal.

And survive he most definitely would, Preston predicted.

All the while currently feeling the demons aggressively snatching him further and further into the depths of hell, fervently weeping and gnashing their teeth.

Chapter 46

After an extremely long night of tossing and turning, Taylor popped up feeling as energetic as a pre-school child who'd almost overdosed on an ample supply of their favorite sugary foods. She bounced throughout the room of her grandmother's home, feeling no regard at all for what she intended to do that day. As if ending a person's existence here on earth was no big deal. To her, Taylor believed that under the current circumstances, it wasn't, especially since certain loved ones were now involved.

She passionately kissed the picture of her father that sat on the nightstand next to her bed, as she prepared herself to leave for the day. She had no earthly clue as to what the day would bring her way. Nor did she attempt to concern herself with the logistics of it all as she went over her plans.

Taylor was such a strategic thinker. She closely observed the details from every possible angle, the good and the bad, just in case she suddenly needed to pivot and make adjustments. This strategy was something that she found herself doing on numerous occasions when it came to dealing with serious matters.

For some odd reason, Taylor felt alive for the very first time in her life, and she couldn't explain exactly why. But she admitted that it felt amazing.

Without realizing that she was smiling, inside and out, Taylor finally caught a small glimpse of her beautiful reflection in the mirror. She meticulously smoothed out her eyebrows with the tip of her index finger, playfully blowing herself a kiss. She gracefully laughed to herself, then turned to leave her sleeping quarters to retrieve the rest of her belongings.

She gathered things that she would need to help captivate the attention of her prey, like lip gloss, her modestly seductive pair of wedge sandals, and her glittery sunscreen that made her skin shine like expensive diamonds.

These items were things that Jezebel would always say were the only things that a true woman of beauty ever really needed in order to grab hold and completely lock the attention of the opposite sex. She would religiously quote these words to Taylor and her siblings.

She pleasurably adorned herself with all of her mother's so-called secret weapons before heading out the door. She walked past a few men and subtly intensified the twitching and twisting of her hips while in their presence. Especially for those that Taylor knew for a fact were dwelling in the alleyways and byways of their community, plotting, planning, and scheming on Preston's demise.

That was something that Taylor just wouldn't allow to happen on her watch, she sacredly vowed.

She spotted the first of Preston's nemesis as they patiently loomed deeply in the shadows of one of the housing project's most unrecognizable crevices. But surprisingly enough, Taylor sadly realized it wasn't a man at all, which placed her in a real pickle. Taylor was not prepared for something such as this. This moment exposed her blatant amateur-like capabilities when it came to dealing with seasoned criminals.

Momentarily stuck in her tracks like a deer in headlights, Taylor had to think quickly on her feet. She knew that her mother was watching her every move and possibly even laughing to herself at the same time.

Taylor instantly changed her direction and headed straight for the vehicle, only to encounter her second set of surprises. Taylor quickly realized that the individual who was devilishly staring back at her with an evil grin was definitely not her mother.

Nor was it Jezebel's car.

She hurriedly pivoted on her heels while trying to make a vast getaway. She knew it was a little too late when she felt Jezebel's deranged young ex-lover's hand aggressively snatching her hair and violently slamming her to the ground, knocking the air out of Taylor's lungs. She struggled to breathe.

A fight ensued as Taylor kicked, screamed, and punched with all of her might. She was hoping that today wasn't the day that the people in her grandmother's community decided to mind their business. If that was the case, Taylor knew that she was done for after staring into the eyes of the crazed maniac. He was slobbering and desperately tried to get a better grasp on Taylor's mouth and neck, to what she believed was to permanently silence her.

Taylor somehow mustered up just enough energy to find his testicles, where she punched, kneed, twisted, and kicked until he screamed out in pain, pissing him off even more. He quickly doubled over in pain, feeling as if his insides were profusely bleeding and swelling before falling to his knees. He was unable to move a muscle, and Taylor, disoriented, scrambled away.

She stumbled and bumped into everything within the alleyway as Jezebel disappointedly looked away, never once peering into the angry eyes of Mystique, whom she blatantly stopped when he attempted to help her very own child. Jezebel couldn't care less about how Mystique felt at the time, especially if it pulled Preston from his hiding place, giving them the advantage of taking his life. Jezebel didn't even care if it meant losing her daughter in the process. She was a cold-hearted being, but that's just how badly Jezebel wanted to see Preston and Taylor gone!

She seductively walked over to her imbecile of an ex-lover and took great pleasure in reopening his long and hideous scar, before snidely wiping his DNA all across his t-shirt as he profusely bled.

Chapter 47

When the *ish finally hits the fan!

Stumbling upon Preston with all sorts of knicks and abrasions, Taylor weakly fell into his arms. Smearing small particles of blood all over his brand-new "The Methods of Talent and Potential" rhinestone tee. Frozen in his tracks, he attentively examined every part of her roughened exterior.

Anger engulfed Preston's entire body from head to toe, but he still could not allow his emotions to get the best of him. As a certain scene from the movie "The Godfather" suddenly entered his mind. The part where the family's opposition ambushed Sonny when attempting to defend his sister's honor after being brutally beaten by her husband.

Preston assessed Taylor's wounds with much precision, vividly recording each nick within his photographic memory bank for when it was finally time to exact revenge on whomever was responsible. He planned to repay the act more than a hundredfold because nobody, and he definitely meant nobody, would ever get away with putting their hands on those that he loved.

Preston tentatively looked at Taylor again before carefully placing her in the care of Lil Gary and Bay, whom he solely trusted to get her home. He knew now for a fact that the *ish was really about to hit the fan. He motioned for his big cousin Jay Jay to accompany him to their secret stash spot, where most of their problem solvers were physically stored.

Jay Jay was a smooth individual who didn't truly like being seen. He only popped up when there was most likely a problem that he loved to correct. In order for Preston to call upon his big cousin and ask for some assistance, things had to be pretty severe.

And as always, Jay Jay willfully obliged.

He once again double-checked his filth-impacted attire, extremely matted wig, and matching beard set before suddenly exiting the car. He didn't go anywhere near the stash house just in case someone was watching, which he figured they most likely were.

Preston filled him in on all the intel about certain things in order to fully bring him up to speed. But what surprised him most was the blatant betrayal of his best friend, Mystique, and how weak he had suddenly become over a woman.

A much older woman who just so happened to be Taylor's mother, at that. Jay Jay unbelievably shook his head in disbelief while giggling at the lack of control from the young man's lust. They had no earthly idea about Jezebel's other previous young ex-lover, who now lay drowning in a pool of his very own blood somewhere close by in an alley. His venomous eyes were finally overtaken by death, while still eerily peering up into Jezebel's deceitful face.

The Grim Reaper suddenly began whispering her name, causing every hair on her body to stand at full attention. Totally freaked out, Jezebel listened as the hollow sounds of the Reaper's voice sent freezing chills clean down the very center of her spine.

"You're next, Jezebel. You're next! So get prepared. Because I have a very special place waiting for you deep in the depths of hell!" The Grim Reaper said, followed by a laugh.

Jezebel witnessed her young ex-lover's profusely jolting body uncontrollably spasm yet again while murmuring her name from the lowest pits of hell before stubbornly taking his last and final breath.

Still looking deeply into her eyes, his body suddenly began losing its natural-born color. That completely freaked Jezebel out to the third degree, as his skin slowly began turning an ashy grey color in hue.

Jezebel was out of breath. Mystique ogled in disbelief, not wanting to believe what he'd just heard or seen. But he honestly did. It was at that very moment that he realized that he was dealing with an entirely different type of entity altogether. Although he physically couldn't prove it. But even if he could, he assumed that no one would believe him.

He tried his best to figure out how to get out of his previous predicament when he realized that Jezebel was far more than just a fine woman with an amazing body and an even larger sexual appetite. Something she splendidly used to her advantage in an exquisitely skillful fashion. In that moment, Mystique fully understood so much more.

He watched Jezebel slowly morph deeper into her darker alter-ego called Sydney Funnel-web in which she was named after one of the world's deadliest spiders. And Mystique agreed that the name fit her perfectly.

He looked her directly in the eyes as she casually made her way back to his side, grabbing his hand. She was pulling him along as if he were no longer the strong and confident young lad that he had once presented himself to be months prior.

There was a coldness in Jezebel's touch that sent chills coursing throughout Mystique's entire frame, making him feel as if he was holding the hand of a corpse. A walking, talking, and deceptively functioning corpse, who would not be denied what she thought was rightfully hers.

She was no longer procrastinating or playing any more cat and mouse games with Preston or Taylor as she headed directly for them both, full steam ahead. In that moment, she had nothing more on her mind other than total chaos, and she didn't care who she had to annihilate to accomplish the task of completely destroying the lives of Preston and Taylor.

But when she arrived at the place where she and her late ex-husband Mark had also been raised, she never expected the outcome she would face. Jezebel found herself on the opposite end of her previous lover's gun. Mystique deviously grinned and winked his eye. He blew Jezebel a kiss as he smirked.

Jezebel stared back at Mystique, unfazed and unresponsive. Her reaction somewhat puzzled him, and another cold chill suddenly came over his physique. But he refused to succumb to his fear. Preston, Lil Gary, and Jay Jay all joined him with a huge smile of their own, each pointing their weapons at different parts of Jezebel's voluptuous frame, cornering off most of the room.

They only left a clear path for Taylor as she and Bay entered.

Taylor looked at her mother but quickly turned away. She couldn't allow Jezebel to see her cry. Instead, she snuggled up against Preston's hardened body for some added reassurance, burying her face into Preston's back as she silently sobbed.

Her heart felt as if it was shattering into a million broken pieces due to the coldness of her mother's eyes. She could visibly see that Jezebel didn't love her. Never had and never would, Taylor comprehended in that moment.

Taylor skeptically removed the small caliber pistol from her waistband and held it at her side. She openly cried, for a million different reasons, as she asked her mother why.

As soon as Jezebel opened her mouth, Taylor hated her response.

Jezebel never once held back her resentment or vengeance when it came to her middle child. The one that she never appeared to love much at all.

"Because you've always taken everything from me," Jezebel venomously spat, angrily pointing her finger in Taylor's direction as she continued to rant.

"First, my husband! Secondly, my dreams! And now my late husband's only son!" Jezebel wickedly laughed in all of their faces, waiting for her response to finally sink into Preston's and Taylor's core as she continuously shrieked with laughter.

She was loving every moment of their highly perturbed faces as they confusedly stared into one another's eyes. Jezebel furthermore explained their imperfect father's infidelity with no fear. Disrespectfully laughing the entire time, until a loud popping sound suddenly reverberated throughout the diminutive space that left all parties temporarily deafened for a brief moment.

Taylor suddenly dropped the smoking gun.

She was crying even harder as she and Jezebel both collapsed to the ground while incoherently murmuring something underneath her breath. Her words sounded something like, "Preston's my brother!" Taylor said those words in disbelief.

She took a good look at Preston through tear-filled eyes as she began seeing the strong resemblance between herself, Preston, and their father, Mark, and she suddenly fainted, steadily murmuring, "Preston's my brother!"

Taylor's body lay there uncomfortably twisted, just like the information that she'd just received.

www.ingramcontent.com/pod-product-compliance
Lightning Source LLC
Chambersburg PA
CBHW032148020726
47496CB00003B/780